Transitional Teaching and Assessment Guide

Sue Bodman and Glen Franklin

University Printing House, Cambridge CB2 8BS, United Kingdom

Cambridge University Press is part of the University of Cambridge.

It furthers the University's mission by disseminating knowledge in the pursuit of education, learning and research at the highest international levels of excellence.

Information on this title: education.cambridge.org

© Cambridge University Press and UCL Institute of Education 2016

This publication is in copyright. Subject to statutory exception and to the provisions of relevant collective licensing agreements, no reproduction of any part may take place without the written permission of Cambridge University Press.

First published 2016

Printed in Poland by Opolgraf

A catalogue record for this publication is available from the British Library

ISBN 978-1-316-60813-5 Paperback

Cambridge University Press has no responsibility for the persistence or accuracy of URLs for external or third-party internet websites referred to in this publication, and does not guarantee that any content on such websites is, or will remain, accurate or appropriate.

....

NOTICE TO TEACHERS IN THE UK
It is illegal to reproduce any part of this work in material form (including photocopying and electronic storage) except under the following circumstances:
(i) where you are abiding by a licence granted to your school or institution by the Copyright Licensing Agency;
(ii) where no such licence exists, or where you wish to exceed the terms of a licence, and you have gained the written permission of Cambridge University Press;
(iii) where you are allowed to reproduce without permission under the provisions of Chapter 3 of the Copyright, Designs and Patents Act 1988, which covers, for example, the reproduction of short passages within certain types of educational anthology and reproduction for the purposes of setting examination questions.
....

Contents

Introduction

    Introducing *Cambridge Reading Adventures*   4

    Overview of Teaching and Assessment Guide   6

1. Teaching reading   8

    What is Reading?   8

    What is Guided Reading?   9

    Reading Fiction Books   12

    Reading Non-fiction Books   14

    Introduction to Book Banding   16

    Book Band Reading Characteristics   18

2. Book by Book Overview   30

    Mapping and Correlation Chart   76

3. Reading Assessment   80

    Completing the Benchmark Assessment Summary   84

    Book Bands Class Progress Tracker   87

    Benchmark Assessment resources   88

Introduction

Introducing Cambridge Reading Adventures

Cambridge Reading Adventures is one of the first Primary reading schemes designed for use by children from all international contexts. To achieve this aim, it moves away from the western-centric approach adopted by many English medium reading schemes. To ensure high quality texts and engaging stories, we went to the very best authors and illustrators from around the world. They have provided an outstanding range and variety of stories and non-fiction, firmly underpinned by a highly successful pedagogy. This pedagogy has been applied by Series Editors Sue Bodman and Glen Franklin of the UCL Institute of Education, ensuring that every page of every book is designed to support the process of learning to read. The series is accompanied by thorough guidance to the teacher, so that every teaching interaction can be planned to develop reading and thinking skills.

Cambridge Reading Adventures provides the young learner with a range of stories, all of which have the kinds of settings, plots and characters which a child growing up anywhere in the world can relate to. This includes a series of stories set in an international school in which the young reader is introduced to the characters Omar, Zara, Hamidi, Beno, Tefo and Leila. Just like the scheme's young readers, Omar and company encounter issues all children will be familiar with such as friendship and disagreement, success and disappointment and even the perils of getting to school. Many stories in the scheme have a contemporary setting designed to reflect life around the world in the 21st Century that the children will recognise, whether at home, in the village or city, or at the supermarket, shopping mall or the beach.

But sometimes the setting is less familiar – with stories about being stranded in a sandstorm or lost at sea.

The scheme also draws on the rich seams of traditional stories from all around the world. The cunning Indonesian mouse deer, Sang Kancil, appears twice, while the legendary Arabic sailor Sinbad also features in two stories. There are traditional tales from China, Africa and other parts of the world.

These are supported at the younger end with a range of humorous stories based around animal characters, like 'Leopard and his Spots' and 'The Hot Day'.

A further rich vein of stories arises in the later book bands with stories based on actual historical settings, such as 'Mei and the Pirate Queen' and 'The Silk Road'.

The use of highly relevant settings and humorous and exciting contexts ensures the teacher can find material that children want to read.

An equally high quality range of non-fiction titles provides balance and breadth to the series. Starting at the very earliest bands, and including information books, reports, recounts and instructional texts, non-fiction titles cover a range of topics of great relevance to the wider curriculum, with full links provided to international curricula in the back of each book. Texts are designed to give the young reader the opportunity to learn the key skills for navigating non-fiction books, and properly utilising features like tables, maps, fact boxes, captions, indexes and glossaries. Teachers are provided with quality materials to teach these skills.

Great care has been taken to choose topics which are directly relevant to the young child growing up in the 21st Century, such as computers, shopping malls, journeying by train and plane and even mobile phone technology. In addition, there is a rich strand of books about the natural world – as it was (such as 'Pterosaur!' and 'Animals of the Ice Age') and as it is now ('All Kinds of Plants', 'Earthquakes' and 'The Great Migration').

For the teacher, *Cambridge Reading Adventures* offers a thorough and dependable teaching structure and comprehensive guidance for teaching guided reading. For a young child learning to read, whether in Bangkok, Dubai, London, Mumbai or Bogota, *Cambridge Reading Adventures* promises a rich, fully supportive and fascinating journey towards becoming an independent reader.

 The UCL Institute of Education's International Literacy Centre (ILC) promotes quality and efficacy in literacy education from age 3 to 13 (Early Years Foundation Stage to Key Stage 3). Over the last 25 years, the ILC, formally the European Centre for Reading Recovery, has successfully trained many thousands of teachers, including those from international contexts, to provide effective literacy teaching through a range of interventions and classroom approaches.

As well as providing high-quality professional support for teachers and teacher educators, the ILC develops materials and professional development opportunities to support teachers to teach literacy skills effectively. One of these is Book Banding, the definitive system for organising texts for guided reading to support early Primary reading, which is currently used in most UK Primary schools. Most recently, Book Banding principles and official listings were published in *Which Book and Why? Using Book Bands and book levels for guided reading in Key Stage 1* (Bodman and Franklin, 2014).

Sue Bodman and Glen Franklin, the Series Editors of *Cambridge Reading Adventures*, are National Leaders at the International Literacy Centre

Introduction

Overview of the Teaching and Assessment Guide

The *Cambridge Reading Adventures Teaching and Assessment Guide* is designed to support teachers to deliver effective guided reading lessons, and to make meaningful assessments that serve to ensure children achieve success.

The Teaching and Assessment Guide is divided into three sections:

Section One: Teaching Reading

This section explores the nature of reading. Based on the underlying principle that reading is a meaningful activity carried out for purpose and pleasure, the range of reading in classrooms is explored and the different features of fiction and non-fiction reading are considered. The nature of guided reading as a specific teaching method is explained. The philosophy and practice of book-banding for guided reading is outlined, with clear examples provided.

This section is predominantly to inform teachers, and provides the theoretical background to the teaching approach employed in *Cambridge Reading Adventures*.

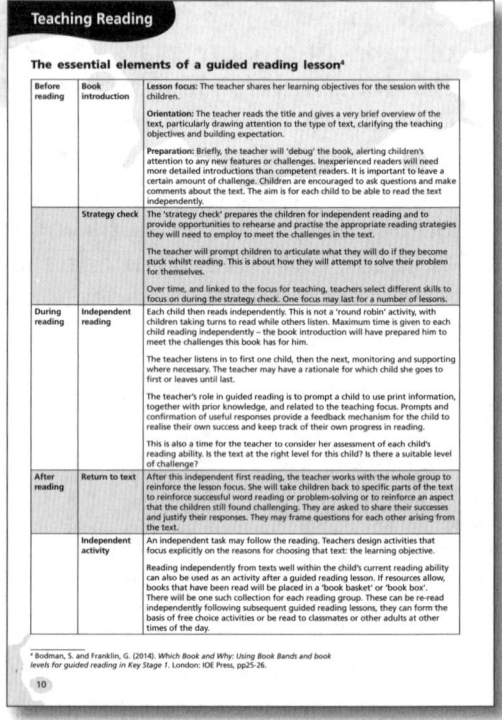

Section Two: Book By Book Overview

Each individual text in *Cambridge Reading Adventures* is explained in detail, helping teachers to select the right book for the right group of children. Teaching guidance is provided for the fiction and non-fiction texts at each band.

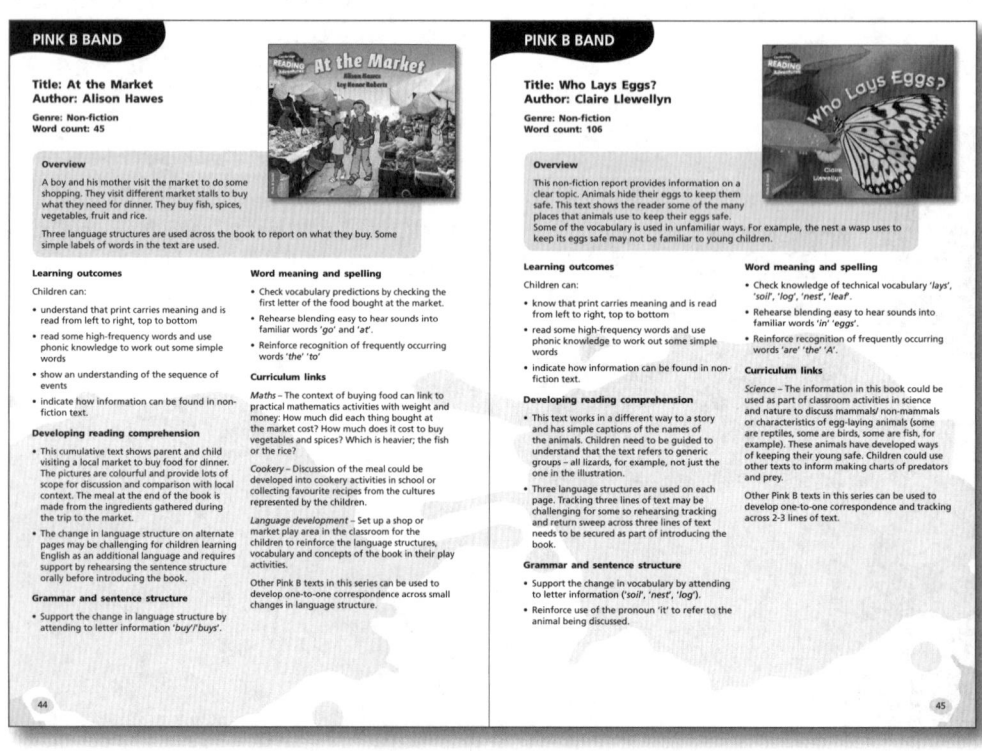

Section Three: Assessment for guided reading

This section offers teachers a benchmark text at each band to support teacher decision-making in assessing whether the child is ready to move to the next band in *Cambridge Reading Adventures*.

A range of support materials is provided for assessing children's reading comprehension. Guidance on how to take, record and analyse running records of text reading is provided. The overall observations are then pulled together as a comprehensive and informative summary of the child's reading behaviour at that band.

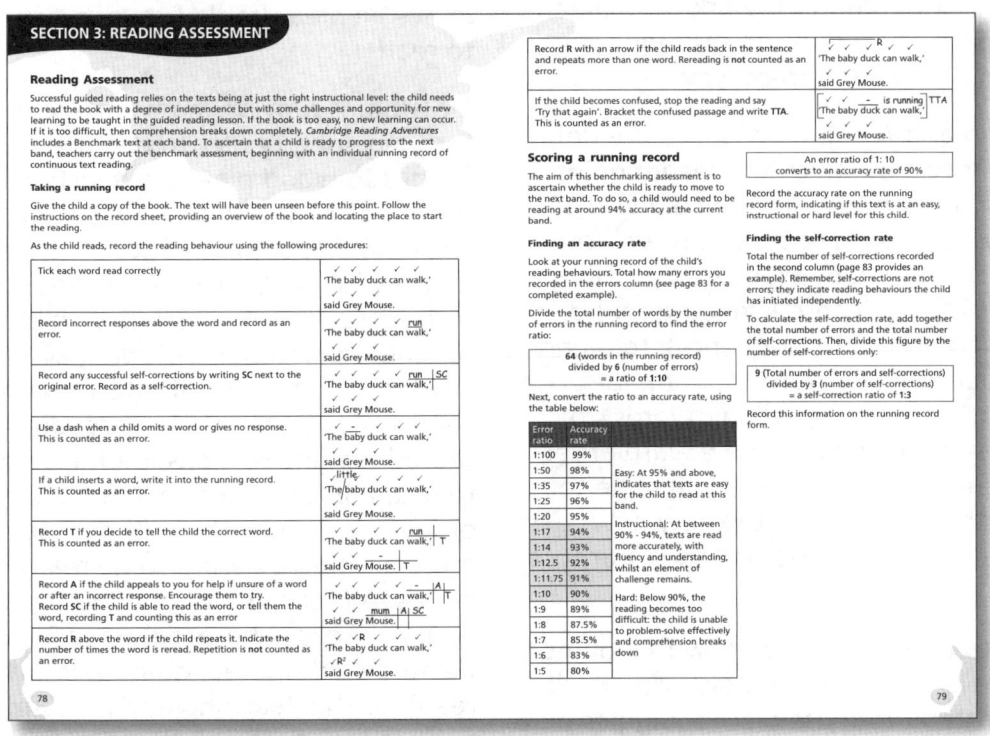

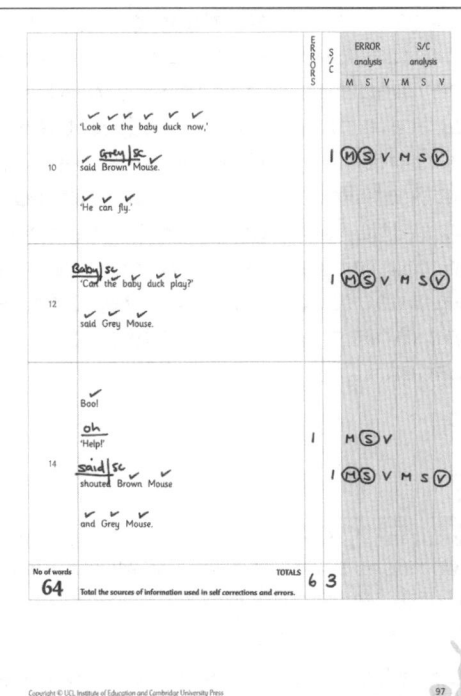

SECTION 1: TEACHING READING

What is Reading?

When you pick up a book, open a web-link or read a set of instructions, what is it that directs what you are doing? You will have had a purpose in mind that shapes how you read and what you do – you might want to settle down and read your new novel, or to check what time your flight is, or you might need to set up your new tablet computer. Sometimes reading will be for pleasure, sometimes for work or to glean information; each of these purposes requires you to read, but in a subtly different way.

In this Teaching and Assessment Guide, we define reading as a process by which the reader gains meaning from the printed word[1]. Reading is a complex act, whatever the purpose: it requires the reader to control many aspects – the ability to match letters to their corresponding sound (grapheme/phoneme correspondence); to blend sounds together to make words; to look for known parts in longer, multisyllabic words; to read sentences, understanding how word order, punctuation and vocabulary choice all serve to convey the author's intention; to know how texts are constructed and to understand their purpose and meaning.

This complex task of reading starts with looking[2]. Beginner readers need to learn how print works. They have to attend to those black squiggles on a white page, to know that they track one-to-one accurately across a line of text from left-to-right in English, to begin to notice letters and words they know, and to understand that what they say has to match what they can see on the page. As children learn more about the alphabetic code, they begin to break the words they can see into separate phonemes, blending them together to read the word. They begin to recognise recurring parts of words such as 'ing' and 'ed' and they link what they already know to the new words they encounter. As more and more words become automatically recognised, reading becomes faster and more fluent. The child starts to sound like a reader.

Young readers seek to make meaning from their very earliest encounters with print. Often the very first word they read is their name. Books for beginner readers provide strong language structures and make good use of illustrations to support meaning. Vocabulary matches the child's oral language. Fiction books have a strong sense of story. Non-fiction books have genuine information to convey. Most importantly, books for young readers are engaging, motivating and above all pleasurable for young children learning to read.

Classrooms provide many different opportunities for the young reader to engage in reading for purpose and pleasure. Teachers read and share stories and rhymes with their children. They provide opportunities for children to read and share books with friends, or quietly by themselves. They make available a wealth of reading material, including access to the Internet and the use of information technology. Teachers demonstrate how reading 'works' in shared reading sessions; perhaps showing how to locate information in a book about animals, or looking at how the author made the story more exciting by using some really interesting words. All teaching of reading requires good quality books, whether the teaching context be modelled, shared, guided or independent reading. This Teaching and Assessment Guide focuses specifically on the use of quality texts in guided reading.

Guided reading operates alongside shared and independent reading in the classroom. The teaching practice of guided reading is underpinned by the work of theorists such as Vygotsky and Bruner. These theories hold that learning is socially constructed through engagement with others. Teachers target their teaching at just the right point in their children's learning, enabling them to do something they would have been unable to do alone. Teachers provide opportunities for children to rehearse this new learning in a supportive, collaborative setting, and expect the children to take on this new learning independently: 'what a child can do with assistance today she will be able to do by herself tomorrow'[3].

---

[1] Bodman, S. and Franklin, G. (2014). *Which Book and Why: Using Book Bands and book levels for guided reading in Key Stage 1.* London: IOE Press

[2] Clay, M. M. (2005). *Literacy Lessons Designed for Individuals – Part 2: Teaching Procedures.* Auckland, N.Z.: Heinemann

[3] Vygotsky, L.S. (1978). *Mind in Society.* Cambridge, MA: Harvard University Press

What is Guided Reading?

Guided reading is a teaching methodology; a way of organising teaching and assessment. It has specific goals. The teacher aims to support the children in reading text for themselves, putting into practice all the aspects of word and letter learning and reading strategies that have been taught previously. To do this, the teacher organises the class into small groups. Each group is carefully matched to a band through assessment. The teacher has a specific learning objective for the group and carefully choses a different book for each; one that helps her guide the learning and thinking of the children in that group. The book offers some challenge to the young readers and, by using awareness of the children's knowledge and experience, careful preparation of the text and the process of literacy acquisition, the teacher offers the right level of support to enable all the children to read the text independently. Active participation at each child's own level of attainment is the aim of guided reading.

A guided reading lesson has some key features:

- Small groups, usually between 4 to 8
- Similar level of attainment in the group
- A copy of the text for each child and the teacher
- A new text in each guided reading lesson
- Reading strategies are applied, reinforced and extended
- The text can be accessed easily (at or above 90% accuracy)
- The children read independently whilst the teacher works with each individual child in turn (as opposed to reading aloud around the group)
- Teacher interactions focus on prompts and praise to support
- From the earliest colour bands, each child is required to think about problem-solving strategies
- It follows a guided learning structure, as follows.

The Guided Reading Teaching Sequence

The guided reading teaching sequence creates:

- an opportunity for the teacher to teach reading strategies explicitly at a text level appropriate to each child.
- an effective and efficient way to provide instruction within a structure which enables the teacher to respond to the range of ability in a class.
- the opportunity for independent reading practice on the right levels of text for each child.
- a context to use and reinforce letters, words and strategies being taught as part of a classroom reading programme, resulting in systematic teaching.
- a focus on reading comprehension.

The table on page 10 gives an overview of the generic teaching sequence for guided reading. All guided reading lessons follow this structure, whether the children are well advanced in the process of learning to read or just beginning to learn. The emphasis and content of part of the sequence will be shaped to support the learner, whatever their current competences.

Teaching Reading

The essential elements of a guided reading lesson[4]

Before reading	Book introduction	**Lesson focus:** The teacher shares her learning objectives for the session with the children. **Orientation:** The teacher reads the title and gives a very brief overview of the text, particularly drawing attention to the type of text, clarifying the teaching objectives and building expectation. **Preparation:** Briefly, the teacher will 'debug' the book, alerting children's attention to any new features or challenges. Inexperienced readers will need more detailed introductions than competent readers. It is important to leave a certain amount of challenge. Children are encouraged to ask questions and make comments about the text. The aim is for each child to be able to read the text independently.
	Strategy check	The 'strategy check' prepares the children for independent reading and to provide opportunities to rehearse and practise the appropriate reading strategies they will need to employ to meet the challenges in the text. The teacher will prompt children to articulate what they will do if they become stuck whilst reading. This is about how they will attempt to solve their problem for themselves. Over time, and linked to the focus for teaching, teachers select different skills to focus on during the strategy check. One focus may last for a number of lessons.
During reading	Independent reading	Each child then reads independently. This is not a 'round robin' activity, with children taking turns to read while others listen. Maximum time is given to each child reading independently – the book introduction will have prepared him to meet the challenges this book has for him. The teacher listens in to first one child, then the next, monitoring and supporting where necessary. The teacher may have a rationale for which child she goes to first or leaves until last. The teacher's role in guided reading is to prompt a child to use print information, together with prior knowledge, and related to the teaching focus. Prompts and confirmation of useful responses provide a feedback mechanism for the child to realise their own success and keep track of their own progress in reading. This is also a time for the teacher to consider her assessment of each child's reading ability. Is the text at the right level for this child? Is there a suitable level of challenge?
After reading	Return to text	After this independent first reading, the teacher works with the whole group to reinforce the lesson focus. She will take children back to specific parts of the text to reinforce successful word reading or problem-solving or to reinforce an aspect that the children still found challenging. They are asked to share their successes and justify their responses. They may frame questions for each other arising from the text.
	Independent activity	An independent task may follow the reading. Teachers design activities that focus explicitly on the reasons for choosing that text: the learning objective. Reading independently from texts well within the child's current reading ability can also be used as an activity after a guided reading lesson. If resources allow, books that have been read will be placed in a 'book basket' or 'book box'. There will be one such collection for each reading group. These can be re-read independently following subsequent guided reading lessons, they can form the basis of free choice activities or be read to classmates or other adults at other times of the day.

---

[4] Bodman, S. and Franklin, G. (2014). *Which Book and Why: Using Book Bands and book levels for guided reading in Key Stage 1*. London: IOE Press, pp25-26.

Guided Reading Record Sheet

Class: Group:

Names:	Date: Text: Band:

Key Learning Goals for the lesson:

Learning Objective and Success Criteria

Planning notes/Key questions/Comments

Child	Notes and observations

Teaching Reading

Reading Fiction Books

Fiction is all about story-telling. As readers, we choose stories that excite, intrigue, puzzle or frighten us. We look for stories that reaffirm our own lives or take us to lives we can only imagine. Haven[5] described stories as 'the primary roadmap for understanding, making sense of, remembering and planning our lives'.

What makes a story? It has been said that there are just a small number of basic story themes, and these have been around since humans first began to tell stories: monsters and villains are overcome; the poor become rich through good fortune or wrong-doing; quests are made to seek to do something or to right a wrong; voyages to unknown worlds are undertaken and the adventurer returns to tell the tale. Stories can be funny or tragic, or a mixture of both.

Sinbad and the Giant Roc, Turquoise band

Fiction writers rework or revise these themes to continue to tell new stories. They intermingle the themes – a quest may have elements of comedy; a monster story might have a rags-to-riches ending. Writers take those basic plots and situations and, by reinventing them, they make it their own.

Yu and the Giant Flood, Gold band

Young children encounter fiction from the earliest age. Long before they can talk, babies and toddlers listen to stories read to them. They demand to hear their favourite books over and over again. From these experiences, they begin to gain a sense of story, implicitly picking up on those story themes. Through hearing stories, they discover how stories work – even the simplest stories employ a structure that moves from a clear beginning to a resolved end. They learn that there are good characters and bad, and begin to empathise with those who are lost or need help. They discover magical lands and faraway places, and look at their everyday world through the eyes of the story teller. The literature-rich school classroom builds upon the story experiences children bring with them from home when they start school.

Jamila Finds a Friend, Pink A band

When writing a book, an author always has the potential reader in mind. A book written to be shared by a parent or carer with a young child sitting on her lap will be a very different sort of book to that which an older reader would chose to read on their own in bed at night. The writer's purpose and audience dictates the style, scope, vocabulary and even the length of the text. The fiction books in *Cambridge Reading Adventures* have been written specifically to be used in a small group guided reading context, led by a teacher, to support the teaching of reading.

---

[5] Page 3, Haven, K. (2007). *Story Proof: The Science Behind the Startling Power of Story.* Westport, CT: Libraries Unlimited.

Reading is, first and foremost, about making meaning. Books for guided reading are designed to support the development of comprehension from the very beginning. The earliest books are short. They have simple language structures that mirror the natural pattern of spoken English. They are illustrated clearly to match the written message, the subject matter is appropriate to children's experiences, and care is taken to choose words and phrases that are within the young reader's own conceptual understanding. Words are phonically decodable or high-frequency, with nouns and verbs supported strongly by the grammar and meaning.

Sang Kancil and the Tiger, Turquoise band

The teaching notes at the back of each book offer guidance to teachers for teaching inference-making in story. Many of the follow-up suggestions provide activities designed to support developing comprehension. This Teaching and Assessment Guide describes each story in detail, and explains the teaching opportunities featured in each individual text as children progress through the banded gradient of challenge (see page 28).

Omar can Help, Red band

As reading progresses, stories require more inferential links to be made. Inference is crucial to reading comprehension. Readers have to move beyond the literal meaning of the actual words on the page, to read 'between the lines' to fully comprehend the author's intention. Kintsch and Rawson[6] describe this as the reader forming a mental or 'situation' model of the story. Readers, they argue, use their prior knowledge, their understanding of the subject and of how stories work, to fill in the gaps. Fiction books in *Cambridge Reading Adventures* have strong story structures to support comprehension. Themes build upon children's own experiences by placing new characters in familiar events, or through traditional retellings of tales from around the world. As books become longer, stories are often sustained over two or more events, or over time. Language structures become more complex, with the meaning sometimes implied by the word order or the author's choice of vocabulary.

---

[6] Kintsch, W., & Rawson, K. A. (2005). Comprehension. In M. J. Snowling & C. Hulme (Eds.), *The Science of Reading: A Handbook* (pp. 209-226). Malden, MA: Blackwell.

Teaching Reading

Reading Non-fiction Books

If we stopped and thought about the reading we have done over the last 24 hours, a large proportion of that reading is likely to have been non-fiction: consulting a recipe book to check the amount of sugar needed; following a set of instructions to load a new computer programme; searching the Internet for the best deals on flights to our chosen holiday location. Non-fiction reading forms an integral part of our daily lives.

Efficient readers modify the way they read according the nature of the text[7]. They will have a purpose when reading it - to answer a question or to find out more information. Reading non-fiction for a purpose is crucial – the reader has to be able to ask 'what do I want to get from this book, and why?'. That is not meant to imply that non-fiction is not pleasurable. A young child who loves dinosaurs will be motivated to read a book about prehistoric animals simply because of that interest. Likewise, reading a good story can lead the reader to want explore the real-life setting or events that provided the stimulus for the plot. However, there are clear differences between story books and books predominantly written for information, and they need to be taught differently.

Pterosaur!, Purple band

Whilst not a definitive list, it is generally agreed that there are six main non-fiction purposes or 'genre' types[8]:

- to recount or retell an event
- to report or describe something
- to instruct or to describe a procedure
- to explain how things work or how they came to be
- to discuss a particular issue, acknowledging different points of view
- to persuade the reader towards a particular position upheld by the writer.

Non-fiction authors, when writing for an experienced audience, rarely delineate so clearly: a book about a farm, for example, might include elements of instruction on how to care for animals mixed with aspects of persuasion about the benefits of organic farming. Non-fiction books written specifically for young children learning to read will present one type of genre very clearly, following the structural organisation and language features that support that purpose for reading. (See the table on page 15.)

Our Senses, Red band

Early non-fiction texts in *Cambridge Reading Adventures* focus predominantly on recounts, reports and instructions. Children's own personal experiences and familiar settings support their comprehension. As reading progresses, texts in the scheme begin to include the other more complex genres, and will move into subject matter less familiar to the reader. Non-fiction features, such as glossaries, indexes, facts boxes, maps and diagrams are gradually introduced throughout, beginning with labels and captions. As each new feature is introduced, teachers need to demonstrate how these are used to support reading for meaning and purpose.

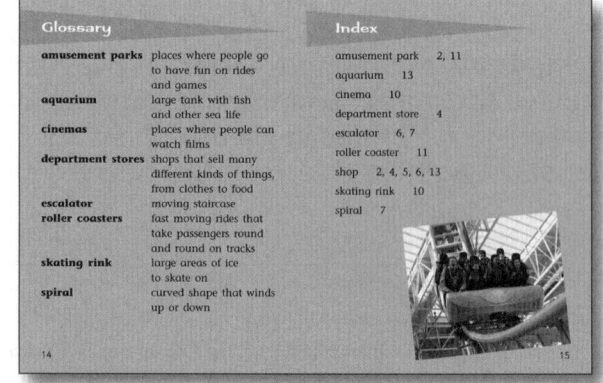

Super Malls, Orange band

---

[7] Wray, D. and Lewis, M. (1997). *Extending Literacy: Children Reading and Writing Non-fiction*. London, UK: Routledge.

[8] Bodman, S. and Franklin, G. (2014). *Which Book and Why Using Book Bands and Book Levels for Guided Reading in Key Stage 1.* London: IOE Press.

Purpose	Structural organisation	Language features
Recount	• A sequence of events written in chronological order	• Written in the first (I/we) or third (he/she/they) person • Past tense verbs to indicate the event being retold has already occurred • The sequence of events is indicated by temporal connectives (first, next, later).
Report	• Commonly non-chronological: the sequence is determined by the component parts.	• Written in the present tense • Addresses the subject generically – not about specific things or people.
Instruction	• Chronologically sequenced steps, sometimes numbered. • May include diagrams	• Uses imperative verbs • Addresses the general reader • May include language of sequence (first, then, after that)
Explanation	• Steps organised in a logical sequence to explain or describe the process • Often use diagrams and cycles	• Written in the present tense • Temporal and causal connectives (because, in order to) used
Discussion	• Presents differing points of view • Draws a conclusion based on the argument presented.	• Written in the present tense • Connectives link the points being made (however, therefore). • Addresses the reader more generally
Persuasion	• Clear statement of the concern to be addressed • Logically sequence leading to a conclusion	• Written in the present tense • Use of powerful, often emotive language to put over the point of view

When using *Cambridge Reading Adventures* non-fiction books in guided reading, teachers select books according to the purpose for reading. They make links with the children's personal experiences and with the classroom curriculum. Good book choice is crucial to support the particular non-fiction reading skill teachers want to teach during the guided reading lesson. The teaching notes at the back of each book offer support for teaching non-fiction reading effectively. Guidance is provided to help teachers decide on the appropriate book choice to meet the needs of their group. Many of the follow-up suggestions provide activities designed to develop non-fiction reading skills.

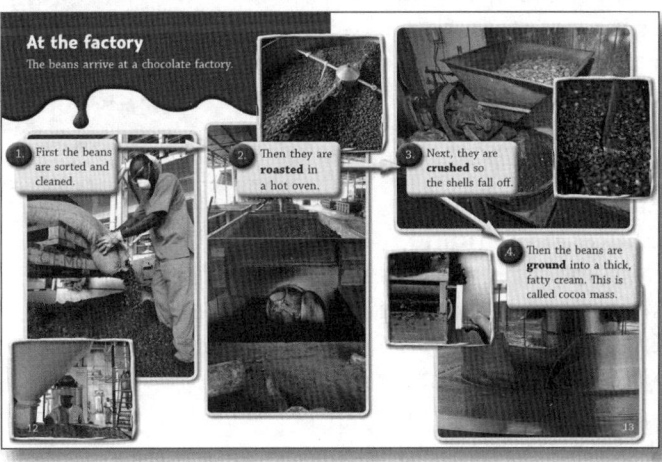

How Chocolate is Made, Turquoise band

Teaching Reading

Introduction to Book Banding

Effective teaching in guided reading needs to offer materials with the right amount of challenge. That doesn't mean finding books with the same letters, words or sentences in, but books that allow the young reader to use what he knows to solve problems encountered in a text. He does this by using the letters and words he does know as anchors to keep hold of the meaning, whilst working out the unknown letters and words for himself. 'Bands' of books are 'collections' or 'groups' of books. Each band shares the text characteristics (for example, phonic complexity of words, grammatical challenges, layout of text on the page, role of the illustrations) and offers the same level of challenge. The stories, the types of text and the sentence structures within each book are very different. Banding offers support for both the teacher and the child, offering consistency of expectation but a range of language and meaning contexts in which to reinforce active reading and problem-solving. It is a way of analysing the amount of challenge in books for guided reading.

Book Banding is also a way of organising books for guided reading. Each band is given a colour and has a clear set of learning and teaching objectives associated with it. Teachers can organise their book collections for guided reading by colour and use that system to monitor and assess progression in reading. Banding has been used successfully for this purpose in the majority of schools in the UK. *Cambridge Reading Adventures* has been banded using the UCL Institute of Education banding system[9], which bands all of the guided reading materials currently in print. This means you can integrate *Cambridge Reading Adventures* into your existing banded resources.

Using bands to group children

Colour bands allow the teacher to be guided by the needs of the child when choosing a book. First, you identify the band at which the child can read with a rate of accuracy between 90 and 94%. Then, you look closely at the assessment record of the child's reading to determine the skills and knowledge that the child needs to learn next. (The section on how to assess reading is on page 80). Then, you choose a text that presents opportunities for learning that link back to the child's needs identified through assessment. By finding the instructional level for each individual child, you can gather together a small group of children working at the same band and work with them in a guided reading context.

Using bands to extend reading mileage

When you know which book band the groups of children in your class are working at, you will be able to select books at the same band with confidence, knowing that they are the right level for each group. Having the choice of lots of books within the child's reading competence will mean that you now choose books for children to read for pleasure in independent reading times. You can do this by selecting stories and texts that are the band below the one you are using for guided reading lessons. For example, children reading at Blue band in guided reading will be able to access Yellow band texts with ease; they will be ideal for independent reading and free choice reading activities.

Selection of Pink A books

---

[9] Bodman, S. and Franklin, G. (2014). *Which Book and Why: Using Book Bands and book levels for guided reading in Key Stage 1*. London: IOE Press

Using bands to support children learning in an additional language

Learning to read in an additional language presents particular challenges. *Cambridge Reading Adventures* supports second language learning in a number of ways:

- Texts provide a good model of English to support the second language learner to hear, practise, and then predict and use in their own reading and writing
- Challenges are carefully phased in order to ensure success and comprehension throughout all reading lessons
- Vocabulary is supported by clear illustrations in both fiction and non-fiction texts
- Introduction of words that need to be decoded is carefully considered to ensure progression in word reading skills
- Links to the wider curriculum are made so that vocabulary and language structures encountered in reading can be reinforced in other subject study
- Guidance for the teacher ensures that language and reading comprehension are at the heart of every guided reading lesson.

Banding Progression

Band	Colour
1A	Pink A
1B	Pink B
2	Red
3	Yellow
4	Blue
5	Green
6	Orange
7	Turquoise
8	Purple
9	Gold
10	White

Bands are arranged into colour groups that support the reader for the very earliest stages of learning to read (Pink band A and B) to becoming an independent reader (White band and beyond).

Bands 5 to 10 are presented here in the Transitional Teaching and Assessment Guide.

The features and characteristics of texts at each band are described in the next section.

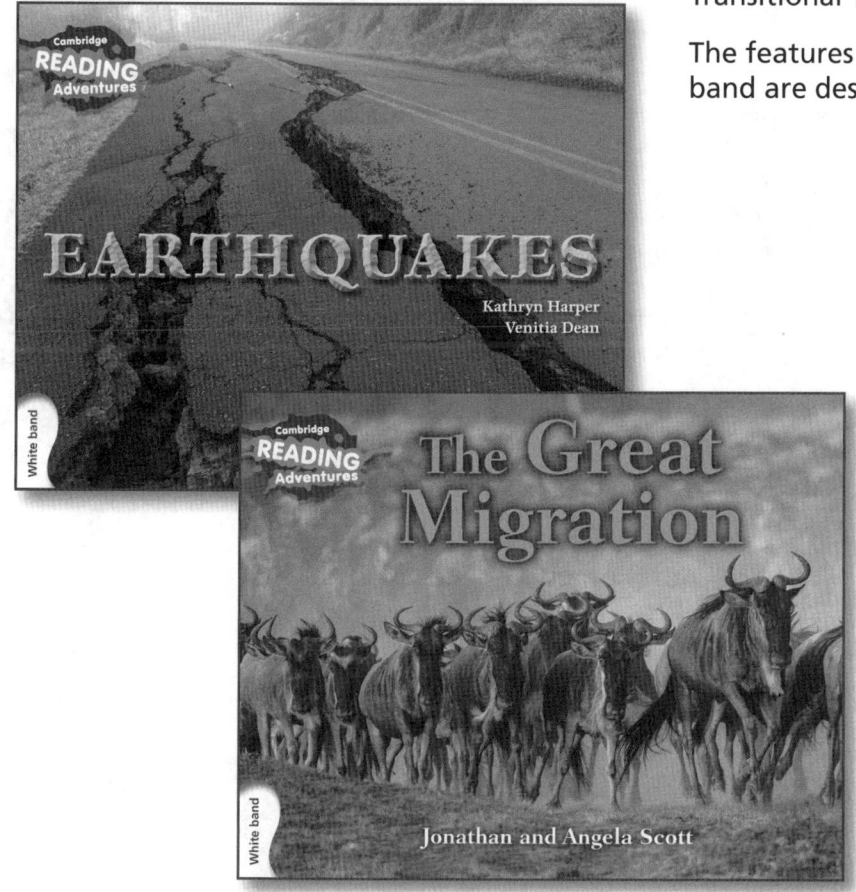

A selection of White band books

GREEN Book Band Reading Characteristics

Green

Green band books provide opportunity for children to read more challenging texts. Texts are 16 pages in length, and have between 150 and 250 words. Children will be reading from an increasing range of styles and text genres, and will be able to distinguish between fiction and non-fiction texts.

An increasing number of lines, from 2 to 6 on a page, supports development of tracking additional lines of print visually and without difficulty. Texts are less repetitive, unless for literary effect. At Green band, the reader can use a range of grapheme-phoneme correspondences to decode unfamiliar words, including common vowel digraphs, whilst ensuring that meaning and syntax are used to support comprehension. Green band texts also offer practice at reading decodable two-syllable words and words with inflectional endings.

Fiction

Stories and events are sustained over several pages, with a wider and more varied number of characters included. More complex story lines provide opportunity for children to discuss and interpret plot and character more fully.

Opening of direct speech is more varied.

There is opportunity to interpret plot and character motive.

Some longer, more complex sentence structures are included.

Take Zayan With You, pages 10-11

Illustrations depict one aspect of the events on the page, providing a more moderate support than at previous bands and necessitating inferential reading of text.

Additional illustrations support comprehension of story line and events.

Non-fiction

Topics relate to the modern world, including situations and events familiar to children. Genres at Green band include recount, report, procedure and some explanation. Texts are authentic, using a variety of picture types and non-fiction devices to inform the reader. Print is located in fact boxes and captions, supplementing information provided in the main body of the text. Children are taught to use the contents and glossary features of non-fiction books in order to locate information and read for purpose.

The introduction of specialised vocabulary is carefully supported by the layout and photographic choices.

Additional information is provided by non-fiction devices such as captions, labels and diagrams.

Baking Bread, pages 4-5

Technical, subject-specific words are defined in the glossary to aid comprehension.

Grammatical structures adhere to the requirements of the specific genre.

There is opportunity to read and consolidate known high-frequency words in a non-fiction context.

ORANGE Book Band Reading Characteristics

Orange

Texts at Orange band provide a more sustained read, with a word count of around 250-300 words. This allows for greater complexity in the writing. A larger proportion of the page is given over to text rather than to illustrations. Increasingly at Orange band, teachers will be prompting children to infer meaning from text through questioning and discussion in guided reading lessons. Children will be able to cross-check information from print, meaning, and syntax, and to self-correct on-the-run.

Fiction

Stories at Orange band support a teaching focus on comprehension beyond the literal, requiring inferential reading. Character motivation is made clear to the reader through detail, language and illustrations. Teachers will be prompting for phrased and fluent reading, drawing attention to punctuation and word choice to support expression.

Word choice supports interpretation, and signals character motive and intent.

Illustrations serve to support the overall meaning, rather than depicting a specific event or aspect of information.

After school, Omar and Beno waited for the bus.

'What's wrong?' asked Beno.

'I ruined Zara's orca. Miss Garcia is cross with me,' said Omar. 'I want to fix it, but how?'

'You'll think of something,' said Beno. 'You always do!'

The next morning, Omar got to school early.

He found some coloured paper and cut out a big rock. He stuck it over the ruined orca.

Omar in Trouble pages 10-11

Longer, more complex sentences are represented, including adverbial phrases and demonstrating use of punctuation.

More literary-style phrases are used.

Sequences of events occur over time, signalled by time connectives and requiring inference to establish causal links between events.

Non-fiction

Non-fiction texts at Orange band contain more formal sentences and include an increasing range of unfamiliar terms. Readers need to pay additional attention to the information located in captions, fact boxes and diagrams to support comprehension. Children are expected to be able to examine non-fiction text layout, cross-checking the information in the text with illustrations and commenting on the content.

Headings are used as a device to support text comprehension.

Glossary words are identified to support reading for meaning.

Sentence structures used are appropriate to text purpose and intent.

SAVING THE REEF

Coral reefs are special. We must look after them. Don't drop your anchor on the reef. It will break the coral.

broken coral

Don't throw your rubbish in the ocean. The creatures may swallow it and die. **Marine** reserves will save our coral reefs. We can look at the marine life but nothing can be taken or touched.

A big storm has washed this rubbish up on the beach.

Life on the Reef pages 20-21

Words or phrases in labels are contrasted with captions.

Clear photographs illustrate and support the points made in the text.

Captions are fully punctuated and add additional information to that provided in the text.

TURQUOISE Book Band Reading Characteristics

Turquoise

Readers at Turquoise band will be developing sustained reading so sentences are more complex and the text is written in paragraphs over longer stretches. Children will encounter a higher ratio of new and more complex words, and will be required to use their known vocabulary, phonic knowledge, and syllabification to problem-solve successfully. Response to reading is an expected part of the guided reading lesson, with children being able to offer opinions on the effectiveness of the book. Books are written to support this type of discussion, with opportunity to evaluate texts, consider authorial intent and relate both fiction and non-fiction texts to their own experiences.

Fiction

Stories now feature more elaborate episodes and events, often with the inclusion of short chapters. There are more extended descriptions, supporting discussion about character motive and reasons for plot outcomes. There is more evidence of literacy phrasing being used in the range of fiction texts (traditional tales and stories with contemporary settings).

- Text layout and line placement aids reading for meaning and supports inferential links between characters and events.
- Texts feature longer, more complex sentences, including adverbial phrases.
- Stories reflect children's interest and experiences.
- Reading and spelling words with affixes

Power Cut pages 16-17

- Children monitor their own reading, using questioning and prediction to support their comprehension of the text.
- Illustrations provide a much lower level of support in fiction texts, focusing on specific details in the text and some of the main events only.
- Specific styles of punctuation are used to support expression and fluency in reading.

Non-fiction

At Turquoise band, children begin to approach different genres with increasing flexibility. They will be able to identify the subject, and consider the purpose and audience of each text. Non-fiction books at this band help children to understand and use the key structural features. Texts include a wider variety of non-fiction organizational devices such as arrows, lines and boxes, to indicate sequences and relationships. Teachers will support children to identify simple questions, referring to the text to find the answers.

Sentences are longer and more formal.

Pronouns require anaphoric resolution to ensure meaning is maintained.

New vocabulary is supported by context and syntax, and with reference to the glossary.

How Chocolate is Made pages 8-9

Format and layout can be evaluated for effectiveness.

Additional information serves to support comprehension.

Multi-syllabic words can be read by identification of known parts and recognition of affixes.

PURPLE Book Band Reading Characteristics

Purple

Books at Purple band are written to support growing independence to predict content, outcome and story development. Text layout varies across a book, often informed by story action or point of information to be made. Illustrations support one aspect of information on each page, with a range of illustration styles across the band. Readers at Purple band will need to adapt to fiction, non-fiction, and poetic language with growing flexibility. Readers may be reading silently. Establishing cause and effect becomes a feature of guided reading lessons at this band. By Purple band, most high frequency words will have been encountered. Children will be solving most unfamiliar words 'on the run' making use of a wider range of word-reading skills.

Fiction

Storylines are increasingly more involved. Children begin to note the way the writer is positioning the reader through word choice and use of literary effects. Characters are defined, enabling discussion of traits and motive to be considered. Some books have short chapters for more sustained reading. One or two pages in a book may have full text with an illustration on the facing page.

Grammar, punctuation and characterisation support children to read with intonation and expression.

Events occur over time and in a logical sequence.

Children's own experiences, such as being lost or frightened, are portrayed in novel or unusual settings.

Then the sands lifted into the sky and the sun came out.

Shan peeped out from under his sweatshirt. 'The storm has gone,' he said. 'You can open your eyes now, Jia.'

Jia uncovered her face. She looked up at the sky and smiled.

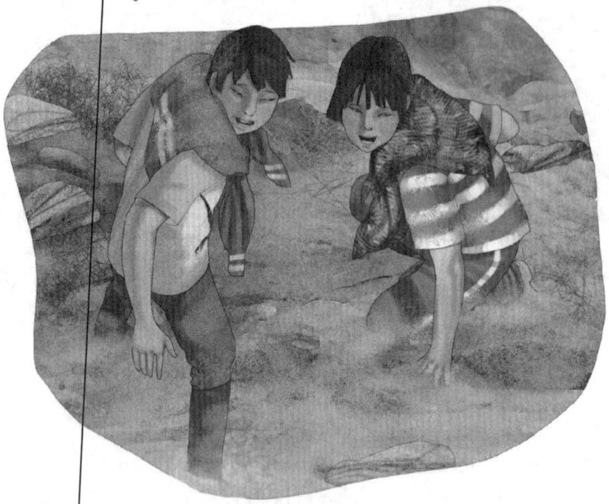

18

'I hope the horses are okay,' she said. Jia went over to where Shan had tied them to the tree.

Both horses looked calm.

'Oh, they're fine,' she said, rubbing sand from their heads.

Shan patted the horses. 'You were both so brave,' he told them.

'Kids, we're over here,' Mum and Dad shouted.

19

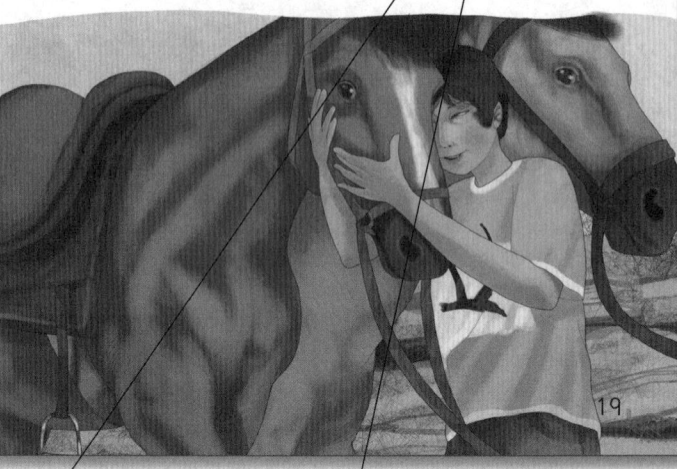

Sandstorm pages 18-19

Longer words are read with attention to syllables and morphological units.

Not all aspects are illustrated and children will need to make inferences based on previous knowledge gleaned from the text.

Sentence structures are becoming longer and more complex.

Non-fiction

At Purple band, readers will be familiar with the formal language of a variety of non-fiction genres. Texts are still well supported by the illustrations, and a widening range of non-fiction text features are employed to summarise information. Non-fiction texts cover an increasing curriculum range and different text formats, and often employ a mixed-genre approach to convey their message.

The appropriate verb tense is used to support the text genre.

A range of different non-fiction features can be used across a two-page spread, each one having a distinct purpose.

Layout and positioning of text varies throughout the book, requiring the reader's careful attention.

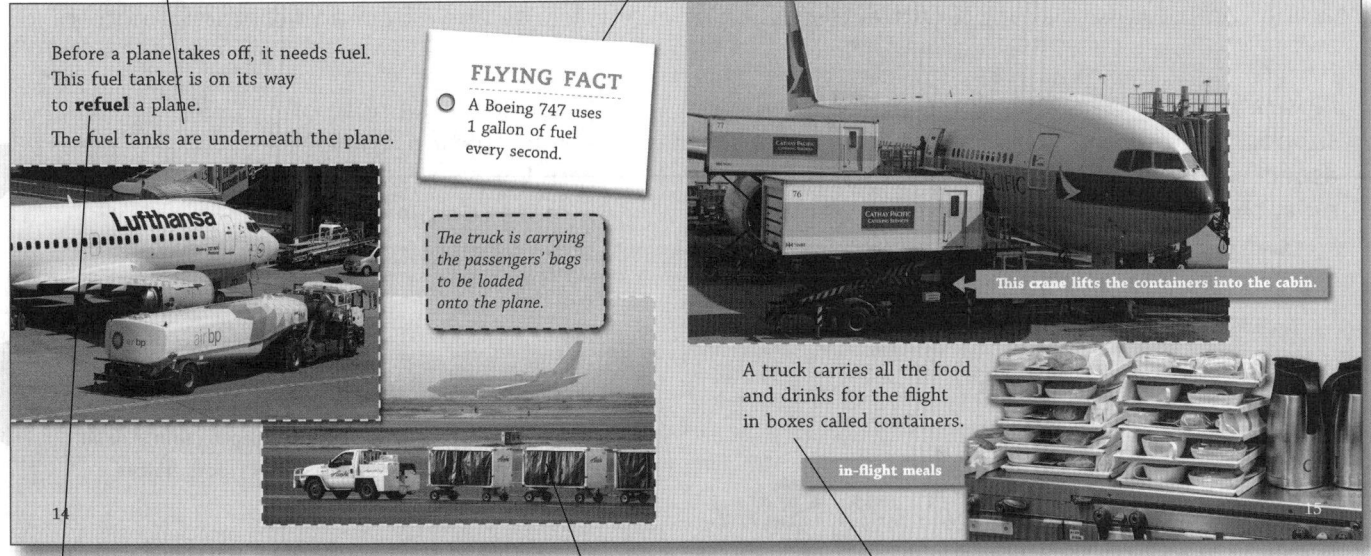

Going on a Plane pages 14-15

Specialist vocabulary is defined in the glossary, listed in alphabetical order.

Readers are able to comment on layout, considering its effectiveness for the purpose and content of the book.

Sentences can be 2-3 lines long, with several clauses.

GOLD Book Band Reading Characteristics

Gold

Readers at this band will demonstrate ability to adapt their reading strategies and behaviours to a range of different styles and text types. A range of illustration styles is evident across the band. Layout and position of text on a page will vary across a book, informed by purpose and intent. Children are expected to evaluate texts and their effect on the reader. Sentence structures are becoming longer and increasingly more complex. For the reader, decoding is now mainly automatic and accurate. Word choice is carefully considered. Unfamiliar words are solved 'on the run', supported by text features, syntax and context. At Gold band, the young reader is beginning to read silently most of the time.

Fiction

Story-lines are more involved, enabling children to speculate about the feelings and intent of the author. Characters are more distinctive and well-rounded than in previous bands. Teachers in guided reading can use this to support critical discussion of events, cause and effect and character motive.

- Illustrations support just one aspect of the story on each page.
- Some fiction books are organised in short simple chapters to support sustained reading.
- Readers take note of punctuation, using it to keep track of longer, more complex sentences.

'Come!' Mr Mars shouted. The boys gathered around him. 'I have chosen the two boys who will join the Lions. They are Pelo and Tefo!'

'Well done, Tefo,' said Omar, even though he was disappointed.

Would Tefo keep playing so well now he was in the team?

10

Chapter 3

Tefo was so happy. Now he was part of the Lions.

'Well played, Tefo,' said Pelo. He shook Tefo's hand. 'But you should buy a new pair of boots before the game,' he said.

Tefo said nothing. He would never get rid of his lucky football boots.

11

Tefo and the Lucky Football Boots pages 10–11

- Sentence length and structure is varied for effect and impact.
- Characterisation is inferred through the author's word choice and use of sentence structure.
- Authorial effect used to engage and challenge the reader.
- Information in the text requires the reader to draw a conclusion and predict an outcome.

Non-fiction

Books at Gold band provide opportunities for children to investigate and make full use of non-fiction layout. Texts include a wide range of non-fiction features such as captions, headings, sub-headings, chapters and textboxes. Information is displayed in different ways, supporting children to locate and interpret particular points. Books are still fully illustrated. The non-fiction texts cover an increasing curriculum range, requiring children to begin to move beyond their prior experience, whilst making links with what they know. Some non-fiction texts at Gold band offer a more compendium-style approach, supporting development of skimming and locating skills, and of posing questions for further research. Children will be expected to be able to evaluate the usefulness of a text for its purpose.

Headings help children to speculate about what the content will cover, and to evaluate the usefulness of this section for research.

Unfamiliar, subject-specific words can be read on-the-run using appropriate reading strategies.

Sentences are written in a format and style appropriate to the genre.

Animals of the Ice Age pages 18-19

Meaning is supported by glossary definitions.

Additional information is provided in facts boxes.

Deductive inference is required to interpret information provided in the text and illustrations.

Scope is provided for discussion and speculation about content, supporting a questioning stance to non-fiction texts.

WHITE Book Band Reading Characteristics

White

White band books encompass a range of genres and writing styles. Books are longer and may not always be read in one sitting. Readers at White band will now be choosing to read silently. At this band, sentences are increasingly complex, often with two or three clauses. Readers need to attend to punctuation to support reading with appropriate expression and intonation. The subject matter chosen at this band provides suitable opportunity for children to express opinions about what they have read, giving rationales and supporting with information from the text. Children now have a large body of known words which can be read by sight. White band books allow children to use the orthography of these words to solve unknown words in their reading, checking the meaning of these through contextual clues, and in dictionaries or glossaries.

Fiction

Characters are more fully developed in the story, and may express contrary views to other characters. Fiction books at White band provide opportunity for children to discuss their interpretation of the text, comparing and contrasting with other texts they have read.

> The storyline may be sustained over a period of time requiring the reader to use connective inferences.

> Illustrations support just one aspect of the story on each page.

> Some sentence structures are longer, with subordinate phrases or clauses.

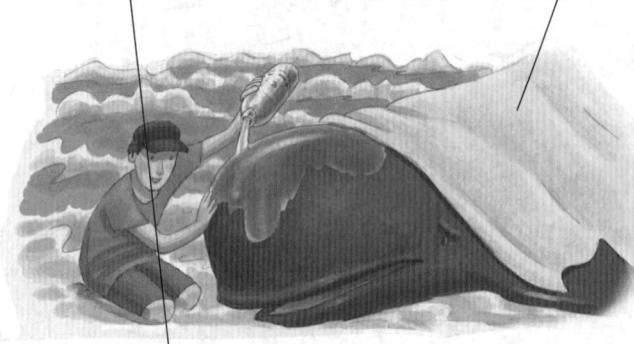

After a little while, the police came down to the bay.
They brought more helpers with them.
Everyone worked hard to try to keep the whales cool and protect them from the sun.
16

A few hours later, the tide came all the way back in.
Everybody rushed to help the whales back to sea.
Selma took in a deep breath and stepped into the sea next to a whale.
The whale she was helping looked distressed.
17

The Great Escape pages 16-17

> Character feeling is implied through word choice rather than explicitly stated.

> Particular words or phrases are used to convey meaning and create effect.

Non-fiction

Non-fiction books at White band use many different types of illustration and ways to summarise content. Detailed information is included. More complex non-fiction features are incorporated, including a range of tables and the use of maps and charts. Children at this band are now beginning to search for and find information easily in non-fiction texts.

Grammar and sentence structure reflect the genre style.

The device of a talking 'expert' adds a personal perspective and enables children to express their own opinions more freely.

Page layout is varied and includes a range of supportive text features.

Earthquakes pages 12-13

Causal inference is required of the reader to make the connection here.

Longer sentences are included, with appropriate punctuation.

Specific technical language is used.

SECTION 2: BOOK BY BOOK OVERVIEW

Title	Band	Fiction / Non-fiction
Take Zayan with You!	GREEN	F
Hide and Seek	GREEN	F
The Lion and the Mouse	GREEN	F
Turtle is a Hero	GREEN	F
Baking Bread	GREEN	NF
Big Bugs	GREEN	NF
A Drop of Rain	GREEN	NF
Dressing for the Weather	GREEN	NF
Omar in Trouble	ORANGE	F
For Today, For Tomorrow	ORANGE	F
Sang Kancil and the Crocodile	ORANGE	F
The Great Inventor	ORANGE	F
The Best Little Bullfrog in the Forest	ORANGE	F
Life on the Reef	ORANGE	NF
Super Malls	ORANGE	NF
Town Underground	ORANGE	NF
The Power Cut	TURQUOISE	F
Sang Kancil and the Tiger	TURQUOISE	F
Sinbad Goes to Sea	TURQUOISE	F
The Great Jewelled Egg Mystery	TURQUOISE	F
How Chocolate is Made	TURQUOISE	NF
Draw the World!	TURQUOISE	NF
Motorcycles	TURQUOISE	NF
Clever Computers	TURQUOISE	NF
Sandstorm	PURPLE	F
Sinbad and the Giant Roc	PURPLE	F
King Fox	PURPLE	F
Going on a Plane	PURPLE	NF
Ships, Boats and Things that Float	PURPLE	NF
Pterosaurs!	PURPLE	NF
The Book of World Facts	PURPLE	NF
Tefo and the Lucky Football Boots	GOLD	F
Yu and the Great Flood	GOLD	F
Lost at Sea	GOLD	F
Animals of the Ice Age	GOLD	NF
Scarface: The Real Lion King	GOLD	NF
Giants of the Ocean	GOLD	NF
Rags to Bags	GOLD	NF
The Great Escape	WHITE	F
Mei and the Pirate Queen	WHITE	F
The Silk Road	WHITE	F
Earthquakes	WHITE	NF
The Great Migration	WHITE	NF
Sticks, Bricks and Bits of Stone	WHITE	NF
The Mobile Continent	WHITE	NF

GREEN BAND

Title: Take Zayan With You!
Author: Peter Millett

Genre: Fiction
Word count: 220

Overview

Zayan and his brothers, Rehan and Aahil, go to the seaside with their parents. His big brothers have to take Zayan with them when they go off to play on the beach. They want to surf or skateboard but Zayan is too frightened of the waves to surf, and skateboarding is too hard for him. Then Zayan discovers he can sandboard. The twist in the story is that this is something his brothers can't do and now Zayan is the one who has to take them with him!

Some children will live in regions without access to the sea, so this setting and context will be unfamiliar. Teachers may wish to share non-fiction texts or on-line video footage of surfers and skateboarders to set the scene for this story.

Learning outcomes

Children can:

- track accurately across multiple lines of print without pointing
- solve new words by identifying known chunks with words, whilst attending to context and grammar
- discuss character motive and explain reasons for actions.

Developing reading comprehension

- It is not overtly stated that Zayan is the younger brother. Inferential reading is required to establish why the brothers need to look after Zayan and why they have to stop their chosen activities because Zayan is unable to join in.
- The illustrations provide additional information and support causal links (for example, on pages 12 and 13, where the brothers are shown being unable to sand board).

Grammar and sentence structure

- Contractions ('*Can't*', '*Let's*') reflect natural speech patterns.
- Varied, longer sentences with adverbial words and phrases ('*today*', '*again and again*').

Word meaning and spelling

- Multisyllabic words ('*skateboarding*') require children to identify parts on words.
- Topic-specific words ('*sand dunes*', '*surfing*').

Curriculum links

Science and Nature – The story could provide the start for work on forces and momentum.

Social Science – Looking after siblings, and caring for each other. Also, that different people have different strengths and skills that we value.

GREEN BAND

Title: Hide and Seek
Author: Lynne Rickards

Genre: Fiction
Word count: 169

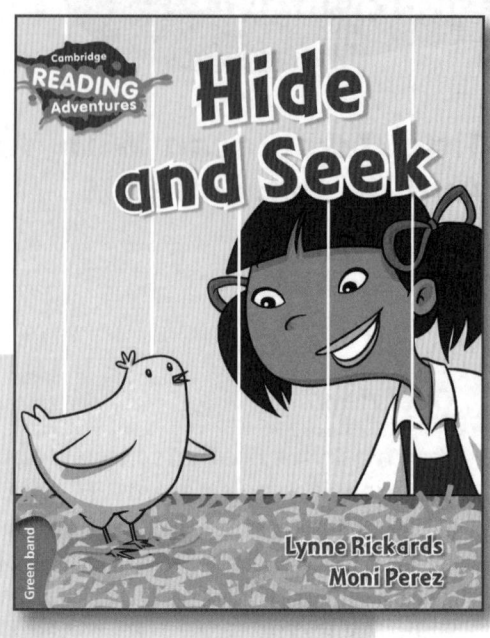

Overview

This story is one of the International School strand of *Cambridge Reading Adventures*. The children in the class are looking after three little chicks called Fluff, Puff and Scruff. It is Zara's job to count them and feed them every day. One day, she counts them and can't find Scruff. The cage door is left open, and the children assume that the chick has escaped. Everyone looks for it. The relevance of the title becomes clear at the end of the story. After searching the classroom, Miss Garcia hears a noise coming from the cage. The children discover that Scruff had never left the cage after all: he was playing 'Hide and Seek'.

Children are likely to be familiar with the characters and setting of this story, as there are several adventures featuring Omar and his friends in earlier bands, for example, 'Omar's First Day at School' (Pink B band) and 'A Day at the Museum' (Blue band).

Learning outcomes

Children can:

- read fluently with attention to punctuation
- discuss and interpret character
- solve new words using print detail while attending to meaning and syntax.

Developing reading comprehension

- Ensure the children understand the game 'Hide and Seek' and can explain how this applies to the story.
- The reader has to infer that the chick has not left the cage, using clues in the illustrations (such as the position of the environmental sounds at the back of the classroom).

Grammar and sentence structure

- Using speech marks and print details (bold print, for example) to inform reading with expression.
- Use of an abstract pronoun; *'There was a noise.'*; *'There she is.'*; *'There it was again.'*

Word meaning and spelling

- Synonyms for talking; *'called'*, *'said'*, *'and'* their link to meaning.
- Decoding words with 3 letter consonant blends; *'Scratch'*, *'Scruff'*.

Curriculum links

PSHE – Taking care of animals would link well with this book. Discussing how to care for animals properly, the importance of feeding and exercise routines, and talking about people who care for animals, would all make helpful links with the story.

GREEN BAND

Title: The Lion and the Mouse
Author: Vivian French

Genre: Fiction
Word count: 273

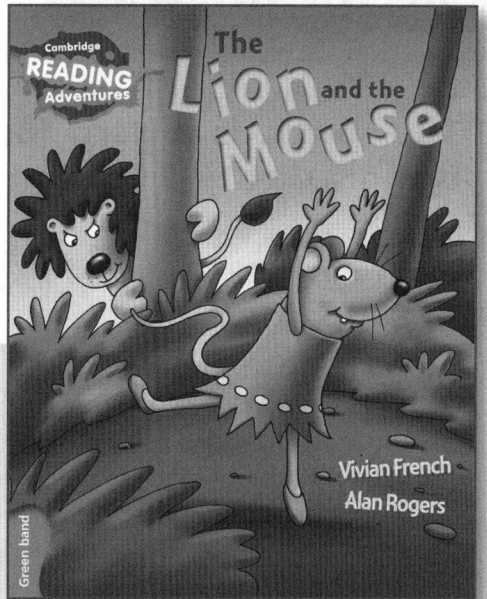

Overview

This story is a modern innovation on the traditional fable of The Lion and the Mouse. In this retelling, we see Little Millie Mouse dancing on her way to her granny's birthday party. On the way she meets Big Billy Lion who wants to eat her! In the end the outcome serves to illustrate the fable's moral, which is that those who are strong can be helped by those perceived to be weak. The layout of the text and the illustrations serve to support meaning and understanding. Some patterned language makes this a fun read for the children.

Learning outcomes

Children can:

- track accurately with their eyes across multiple lines of print
- self-correct own errors using appropriate cue sources, whilst reading with expression and meaning
- discuss plot and character traits with understanding.

Developing reading comprehension

- Children can discuss character motive – why would Big Billy Lion want eat a little mouse? Can they predict how Little Millie Mouse might conceivably help him?
- The story takes place over time and with a series of events which lead to a culmination. Children should be able to retell the events in sequence, and consider alternative outcomes.
- Compare and contrast with the original Aesop's fable of The Lion and the Mouse. What features has the author retained? What is different? How effective is this retelling?

Grammar and sentence structure

- Some limited repetition of structured phrases and unfamiliar words.
- Text effects, such as capitalisation and ellipsis, aid phrased and expressive reading.

Word meaning and spelling

- Simple phonically decodable words which can be solved 'on the run'.
- Use of word play and onomatopoeia for effect.
- Rhythmic patterned words and phrases.

Curriculum links

Humanities - Examples of true life stories of human endeavour and triumph over adversity.

Literacy - Compare and contrast other versions of the same fable, or stories on the same theme. Also, stories from religious texts, such as the tale of David and Goliath.

GREEN BAND

Title: Turtle is a Hero (Benchmark Text)
Author: Gabby Pritchard

Genre: **Fiction**
Word count: 299

Overview

Turtle loves to swim and he likes to sleep on the beach too. One day, Turtle meets a little boy on the beach. At first the boy only notices how different Turtle looks, and thinks he has met a dinosaur. Turtle explains why he is not a dinosaur, pointing out his flippers and his hard shell. Later in the story, this hard shell proves useful when the boy gets into trouble in the sea. Turtle swims out to rescue him, bringing the boy back to shore on his back, and the two become friends.

This story has elements of an often-used idea where a weaker creature helps a stronger one. It offers opportunity for comparison with 'The Lion and the Mouse' in the same band of *Cambridge Reading Adventures* series.

Learning outcomes

Children can:

- read fluently with attention to punctuation
- discuss and interpret character and plot to support meaning.

Developing reading comprehension

- Character motive is important to comprehending the story: why would Turtle help the little boy? Why is the little boy initially wary of Turtle?
- The author gives a clue to future events on page 11 when the boy says: '*I think your hard shell could be very useful*'. Children could predict in what ways the shell might prove useful, confirming their predictions with later events in the story.

Grammar and sentence structure

- Use of descriptive language; '*golden sand*', '*strong shell*', '*deep, green sea*', '*cool place*'.

Word meaning and spelling

- Challenging vocabulary in this context; '*wrinkly*'.
- Reinforce different ways of writing /ee/ words in context: '*deep, green sea*'; '*beach*'.

Curriculum links

Social Studies – This story could link to a topic of People who help us where children research people in the community who help keep them safe. Other stories that deal with strong versus weak would be useful reinforcement to this story, for example, 'The Lion and the Mouse', and 'King Fox' in *Cambridge Reading Adventures*. These stories could be read aloud to the children.

GREEN BAND

Title: Baking Bread
Author: Lynne Rickards

Genre: Non-fiction
Word count: 215

Overview

This non-fiction book explores the process of making bread. It incorporates features of simple explanation texts, such as following a series of logical steps in chronological order.

Young beginner readers are less likely to have experienced this non-fiction genre, as the focus for five and six-year olds is predominantly on recount, report and instruction. This text would be particularly suitable for older learners reading at Green band.

Learning outcomes

Children can:

- read a widening range of new or unfamiliar words, using appropriate reading strategies including decoding of regular words ('*vat*', '*spins*')
- distinguish between a fiction and non-fiction text, naming some key features of non-fiction
- use the index and glossary pages to locate information and support comprehension.

Developing reading comprehension

- Photographs and captions support the information in the text.
- Non-fiction features (glossary, index and labelling) support locating and extracting meaning from text.

Grammar and sentence structure

- Sentences are written in simple present tense, consistent with explanation texts.
- Time connectives ('*Now*', '*It's time*') indicate the sequence of events.

Word meaning and spelling

- Specialised vocabulary is used to describe the bread-making process: '*rise*', '*pounds*', '*vat*'. These words are defined in the glossary.
- Spelling of present tense verbs – adding simple /s/ ending.

Curriculum links

Science and Nature – Cooking activities: explore different types of flour, different methods of cooking, what happens when yeast is added, etc. If possible, you could visit a bakery in your local area.

Literacy – Read stories that feature cooking or baking, such as 'The Gingerbread Man', 'The Magic Porridge Pot', 'Stone Soup'. Innovate on stories read: children could write instructions for making a gingerbread man, for example.

GREEN BAND

Title: Big Bugs
Author: Claire Llewellyn

Genre: Non-Fiction
Word count: 312

Overview

This appealing and attractive non-fiction report provides information about the larger bugs of the insect kingdom. The book provides ample opportunity for children to use the important features of non-fiction texts, such as facts boxes and captions, effectively at this band. A contents page and glossary are available to locate specific information and specific bugs, together with a simple chart. The report is written in the present tense as appropriate for books in this genre.

Whilst the language structures are in the main simple, the technical vocabulary is a challenge for the reader at Green band. It would be useful to address problem-solving strategies for these words before reading the text. Size of the bugs is presented. This will be very appealing to the young reader although measurement of any type presents conceptual challenges.

Learning outcomes

Children can:

- read more challenging texts
- use contents page and glossary in non-fiction books, and locate information
- read decodable two-syllable words
- distinguish between fiction and non-fiction texts
- solve new words using print detail while attending to meaning and syntax.

Developing reading comprehension

- On page 12, it states: *'Most bugs are very small but some of them are GIANT!'* Children will need to make sense of the relative size of these creatures and why they are considered to be 'big' as indicated by the title.
- The chart on page 14 offers facts in a different format, encouraging children to read the information in a different way.

Grammar and sentence structure

- Short sentences that present facts.
- Use of a glossary to define words.

Word meaning and spelling

- Vocabulary of comparative size: *'giant'*, *'longest'*, *'biggest'*
- Decoding using syllables to decode: *'At-las'*, *'in-sect'*, *'Ta-ran-tu-la'*

Curriculum links

Maths – The chart on pages 14 and 15 could support mathematics activities that present summaries of features and characteristics. Similar charts that summaries information about other bugs, or other types of creatures could be developed following discussion of this chart.

Geography – The bugs in the book come from different habitats in different parts of the world. A geography lesson locating them on a world map and researching habitats would provide an interesting extension for children.

GREEN BAND

Title: A Drop of Rain
Author: Tanya Landman

Genre: Non-Fiction
Word count: 205

Overview

This simple explanation text describes the water cycle in a clear and accessible way for young readers. It provides a structure to follow a sequence of events, whilst using a more story-style format to explain the scientific process.

Teachers will need to be sensitive if using this book with children who may have had experience of floods or drought.

Learning outcomes

Children can:

- read fluently with attention to punctuation
- manage effectively a growing variety of texts, including non-fiction
- make predictions about the content
- read decodable two-syllable words.

Developing reading comprehension

- Make links with other cycles that children may be familiar with, such as life cycles.
- Children will need to be able to explain in their own words what happened to the raindrop on its journey to reach the sea.

Grammar and sentence structure

- Ellipsis (three small dots) is used to aid fluency and expression in reading and to add to the build-up of events.
- Several examples of complex sentences which support development of ideas and can be used to explore impact of word order.

Word meaning and spelling

- Use of comparatives ('*bigger*', '*wider*', '*deeper*') as the raindrop moves on its cumulative journey through the cycle.
- The addition of /er/ on some comparative words requires doubling the consonant ('*big – bigger*').

Curriculum links

Science and Nature – The narrative style of retelling a life cycle could be applied to writing other non-fiction explanatory texts. This playing with the genre features can only really be effective after children are familiar with how explanation texts are structured. Other books in the *Cambridge Reading Adventures* scheme explore different types of cycles. See, for example, 'Making a Car' (Blue band) and 'How Chocolate is Made' (Turquoise band). Experiments with water vapour, ice and steam will demonstrate the water cycle.

Maths – Ordering of size related to number, linked to ordering of numbers: bigger than ... or smaller than ... a given number.

Literacy – Collect examples of comparative and superlative adjectives. Present on a word wall or in a class dictionary.

GREEN BAND

Title: Dressing for the Weather
Author: Kathryn Harper

Genre: Non-fiction
Word count: 365

Overview

This simple non-chronological report explores different extremes of hot and cold weather across the world, and the clothing people wear accordingly.

Children will know about different types of weather, depending upon which region they live in. It is important to start by activating prior knowledge of children's own experiences.

Children may have already read 'The Weather Today' (Red band) from *Cambridge Reading Adventures*.

Learning outcomes

Children can:

- distinguish between a fiction and non-fiction text, naming key features of non-fiction
- self-correct errors whilst reading, using a range of cue sources
- use a contents page and glossary effectively to locate information.

Developing reading comprehension

- Several non-fiction devices support the young reader at this band, including captions and some simple maps.
- Layout and design support comprehension through the use of icons and coloured backgrounds.

Grammar and sentence structure

- Sentences are varied in length, including some use of conjunctions, and commas to demarcate lists (such as on page 6: '*They wear thick winter coats, trousers and mittens.*').
- Verb tense is consistent with the features of non-chronological reports.

Word meaning and spelling

- Some less familiar and specific vocabulary used, such as place names and technical vocabulary ('*moisture*', '*equator*').
- Use of adjectives serves to delineate between the extremes of weather ('*loose clothes*', '*thick winter coats*', '*cold wind*').

Curriculum links

Science and Nature – Observe weather patterns over a period of time, charting the types of weather over a particular month or in different seasons. Experiment with different types of clothing materials; for example, which materials are most effective for keeping us warm?

Maths – Chart the weather every day each week. How many days were hot? Which month is the hottest in your region?

ORANGE BAND

Title: Omar in Trouble
Author: Gabby Pritchard

Genre: Fiction
Word count: 360

Overview

This book featuring Omar and his friends is another story in the International School strand of *Cambridge Reading Adventures*. Omar is in trouble: he has ruined Zara's painting and Miss Garcia is cross with him. The story focuses on Omar's attempts to put things right for his friend, and to please his teacher.

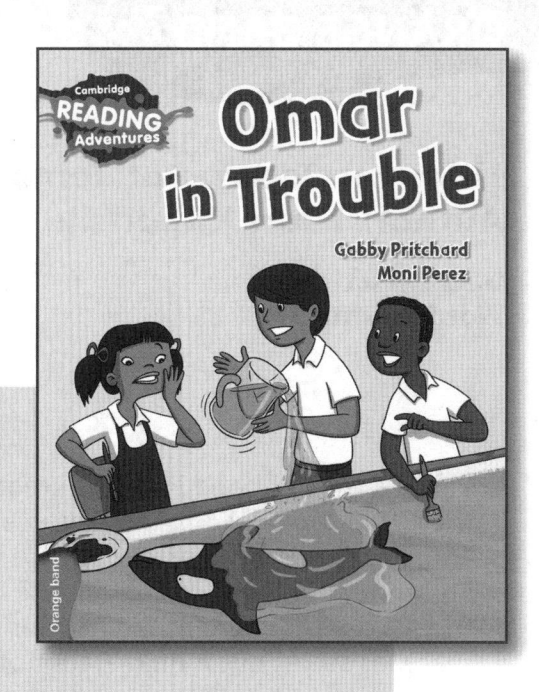

The children are likely to be familiar with the characters in this story, as they feature in several of the earlier bands ('Omar's First Day at School', 'Omar Can Help', for example). Concepts of friendship and helping are recurring themes in this strand, and children will be able to relate to their own experiences.

Learning outcomes

Children can:

- maintain meaning over a sequence of events over time
- apply phonic knowledge and skills on new, unfamiliar words, whilst holding a sense of the story events
- problem-solve longer words by breaking them apart using familiar syllables
- consider events and provide reasons for why they might have happened.

Developing reading comprehension

- Events develop and progress over two days, and the reader has to make temporal links.
- Causal inference is required. For example, if only Omar had used a smaller jug ...
- Identifying problem and resolution in story structure.

Grammar and sentence structure

- Sentence structures are more complex, with two or more idea units.
- More literary structures used (such as: *'I want to fix it, but how?'* on page 10).

Word meaning and spelling

- Wider range of verbs ('*begged*', '*asked*', '*laughed*') to support reading with expression and understanding.
- Longer words require breaking into syllables: '*display*', '*careful*', '*fantastic*'.

Curriculum links

Art – Children could create their own frieze around a class topic. Spilling water on a painting can create some interesting effects – children could experiment!

Science and Nature – Zara paints an orca. Use non-fiction texts to discover more about orcas and write captions for Zara's picture.

ORANGE BAND

Title: For Today, For Tomorrow
Author: Lauri Kubuitsile

Genre: Fiction
Word count: 373

Overview

This is a further book in the International School strand of the *Cambridge Reading Adventures* series featuring Omar and his friends. In this story, Omar's friend Hamidi is saving all his money. He is not telling anyone what he is saving for. His friends tempt him to spend his money and try to get him to share his secret but Hamidi does not tell them. Nor does the reader find out until the very end.

Children are likely to be familiar with the characters and setting of this story, as there are several adventures featuring Omar and his friends in earlier bands for example, 'A Day at the Museum' (Blue band) and 'Hide and Seek' (Green band).

Learning outcomes

Children can:

- maintain meaning whilst reading longer, more complex sentences
- self-correct errors on-the-run by crosschecking information from print, meaning, and grammar
- search for and use familiar syllables within words to read longer words
- recognise when information is not overtly explained in the text, and use appropriate inferring strategies.

Developing reading comprehension

- The title is abstracted. Teacher will need to explain this in the guided reading lesson, linking to children's own experiences of having to wait for something they really want.
- Opportunity is provided for children to consider Hamidi's motive and actions throughout the story: for example, on pages 9 and 10, Hamidi has a dilemma – he would really like to go to the fair, but also wants to save his money. What will he do? What factors help him make his decision?

Grammar and sentence structure

- Longer phrases, and more complex sentences with causal connectives such as 'but' indicating the decisions made by characters.
- Dialogue, indicated by punctuation, is used to move the story forward.

Word meaning and spelling

- Word meanings not directly explained in text, for example: '*carousel*', '*funfair*'.
- Print features for emphasis, such as the use of italics to stress '*your* money' on page 6.

Curriculum links

PSHE – Talk about thrift and budgeting. It could be linked to the school raising funds to purchase new items through holding a fête, for example.

Maths – How long did it take Hamidi to save up for his bike? How much pocket money did he have? Create different scenarios where children could save money to buy different things.

ORANGE BAND

Title: Sang Kancil and Crocodile
Author: Jim Carrington

Genre: Fiction
Word count: 390

Overview

This is a simple retelling of a traditional tale from Indonesia. Sang Kancil is a clever mouse deer. One day, he spies some delicious water apples on the other side of the river. He wants to cross over the river to eat them, but unfortunately, the river is full of hungry crocodiles! Sang Kancil outwits Crocodile by tricking him.

The story follows the format and structure of other traditional tales, for example, the Brer Rabbit stories of the American South, with which children may be familiar.

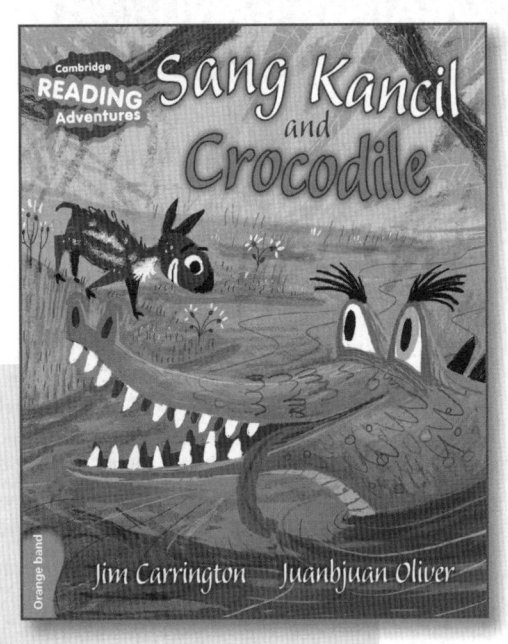

Learning outcomes

Children can:

- infer meaning from the text
- read longer phrases and more complex sentences
- attend to a greater range of punctuation
- search for and use familiar inflectional endings /ed/ to read past tense words.

Developing reading comprehension

- The author indicates through word choice rather than directly telling the reader, requiring inferential reading. For example, on page 6, why is Crocodile licking his lips?
- Characterisation is supported by dialogue and verb choices, enabling the reader to read for meaning and with appropriate expression.

Grammar and sentence structure

- Dialogue between the characters offers opportunity to explore the way punctuation of speech is used as a guide to reading with fluency and phrasing.
- There are examples of longer, complex sentences containing more than one idea, supported by the use of punctuation.

Word meaning and spelling

- The text includes many examples of regular past tense inflectional endings. These endings are often difficult for English language learners if past tense is inflected differently in the first language.
- Specific words and phrases (such as 'sly') support the reader to infer the intention.

Curriculum links

Maths – The crocodiles line up in rows across the river. Practice multiplication skills: there were 24 crocodiles in 6 rows, how many in each row? How would Sang Kancil count them (practising counting in fours)?

Citizenship – Read non-fiction books about crocodiles and where they live. Find out more about the mouse deer, which is also known as a chevrotain, by searching on the Internet.

ORANGE BAND

Title: The Great Inventor
Author: Gabby Pritchard

Genre: Fiction
Word count: 424

Overview

In this humorous story, it is too hot for Kito and his friends to play football. Instead they go to visit Kito's Uncle Juma, the inventor. The Great Inventor in the title turns out to be Kito, as he invents something useful to help them all stay cool.

It is important to establish children's prior knowledge of inventors and inventions. In introducing the book, use the front cover illustration to establish the sorts of things an inventor might do: Why might there be smoke coming out of an inventor's shed? Why might inventors cause explosions?

Learning outcomes

Children can:

- maintain meaning over a sequence of events over time
- apply phonic knowledge and skills on new, unfamiliar words, whilst holding a sense of the story events
- problem-solve longer words by breaking them apart using familiar syllables (for example, 'inventor', 'watering' 'fantastic')
- consider events and provide reasons for why they might have happened.

Developing reading comprehension

- The sequence of events takes place over time, requiring the reader to make temporal connections.
- The main character's problem-solving attitude to getting too hot to play football supports inferential skills as children predict what the outcome might be.

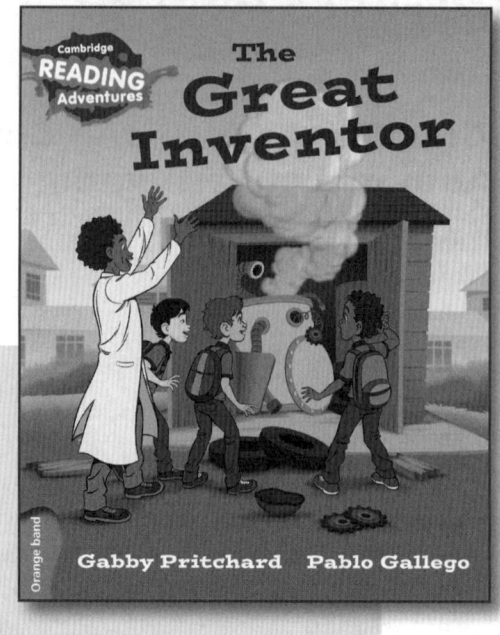

Grammar and sentence structure

- Sentence structures are more complex, with two or more idea units.
- Humour introduced through choice of vocabulary (such as: 'Kid Cooler Machine').

Word meaning and spelling

- Wider range of verbs ('cried', 'sighed', 'laughed') to support reading with expression and understanding.
- Longer words require breaking into syllables (such as: 'display', 'careful', 'fantastic').

Curriculum links

Design Technology – Children could use junk modelling techniques to make their own 'Jumbo Cleaning Machine' or 'Kid Cooler Machine', or maybe one of their own suggestions!

Science and Nature – Children design paper fans and investigate which types of paper and designs are more effective. They could experiment by seeing which fans can move light objects, such as a feather, further. This subject could also support science work on circuits and electricity, where children design working fans.

ORANGE BAND

Title: The Best Little Bullfrog in the Forest (Benchmark Text)
Author: Ian Whybrow

Genre: Fiction
Word count: 651

Overview

This humorous story focuses on a little bullfrog who wants to be the best at something. The animals of the forest compete with each other at a talent contest and the little bullfrog is left feeling disheartened. In this story, the little bullfrog so wants to be the best at something. He can't compete with the other animals when it comes to singing, flying, looking beautiful – or even being smelly and disgusting. But of course, his mother loves him best of all and wouldn't want him any other way.

Learning outcomes

Children can:

- search for and use familiar syllables within words to read longer words
- read longer phrases and more complex sentences
- attend to a greater range of punctuation and text layout.

Developing reading comprehension

- The reader needs to understand why little bullfrog tries to compete and why his mother seems unconcerned that he isn't beautiful and can't sing.
- Inference is supported towards the build up through the story, as events build towards the conclusion where little bullfrog recaps on all the things he can't do.

Grammar and sentence structure

- Increased amount of direct speech requiring use of punctuation to read fluently and with expression.
- Literary phrase; *'and with that'*.

Word meaning and spelling

- Challenging vocabulary; *'slithering'*, *'charged'*, *'flicked'*, *'mighty'*
- Decoding novel words in context: *'swish'*
- Final *y* in adjectives; *'lumpy'*, *'ugly'*, *'nasty'*, *'mighty'*, *'smelly'*.

Curriculum links

Science and Nature – This story lends itself to links with project work on animals. The animals in the story have a range of talents and abilities. Pupils could use non-fiction texts to create profiles of their favourite animals, describing what each animal can do. This would enable pupils to experience the differences between writing fiction and non-fiction texts. Further reading in this series that would like to this story includes; 'Big Bugs'; 'Life on the Reef'; 'Giants of the Ocean'.

ORANGE BAND

Title: Life on the Reef
Author: Andy Belcher

Genre: Non-fiction
Word count: 380

Overview

The coral reef is teeming with life. This non-fiction report provides the opportunity for children to learn about life on a coral reef. Enjoying the stunning photography, children can find out about the many creatures that make this underwater world their home. The text provides opportunity for children to practise using a range of non-fiction text features to support their reading and understanding of the information provided, through the use of captions and labels for, example.

Learning outcomes

Children can:

- infer meaning from the text
- read longer phrases and more complex sentences
- attend to a greater range of punctuation
- search for and use familiar inflectional endings /ed/ to read past tense words.

Developing reading comprehension

- Children have the opportunity to pose questions and locate information using non-fiction text features to support the answers given.
- The text tells the reader '*Coral reefs are special*' (page 20). What do the children understand is special about coral reefs? Inferential reading is required for children to be able to substantiate this statement.

Grammar and sentence structure

- Sentence structures are more formal than those used in fiction texts at this band, using language common in the report genre.
- Longer complex sentences often provide more than one piece of information.

Word meaning and spelling

- The text uses many pronouns ('*this*', '*these*', '*they*'). The precise interpretation of the subject of these pronouns may be challenging for some learners, particularly those learning English.
- Technical vocabulary associated with the topic is used. Although well supported by illustration, understanding of this vocabulary may need supporting when introducing this text.

Curriculum links

Art – the stunning photography in this book provides the opportunity to follow up the reading with observational drawings. These could then be labelled using the information in the book.

Geography – page 4 tells us where in the world reefs can be found. Choose one of those areas and find out more about it. What fish can be found there? Are there any wrecks? Find out more from the Internet.

ORANGE BAND

Title: Super Malls
Author: Anita Ganeri

Genre: Non-fiction
Word count: 293

Overview

Malls have lots of shops but in a super mall people can do a lot more than just go shopping. This non-fiction report text investigates the many different things people can do in a super mall. Some incredible malls are pictured from around the world.

Shopping is a familiar activity for most children. However, not all will be familiar with the types of super malls described in this text. Establishing children's prior knowledge and experience will be important for the guided reading lesson. Help children to make links with what they know of shops and shopping with super malls described here.

Learning outcomes

Children can:

- use a variety of non-fiction page layouts
- problem-solve longer words by breaking them apart using familiar syllables
- use illustrations to check information in the text.

Developing reading comprehension

- A clear non-fiction layout provides opportunities for the young reader to become familiar with how to use a contents page and an index.
- Subject-specific understanding is support by photographs, and by the use of a glossary to establish word-meaning in context.

Grammar and sentence structure

- Sentence structures include the abstract pronoun (for example, 'There are malls all over the world.' on page 3; 'There are all sorts of shops in a mall.' on page 4).
- Some sentences are long and complex (such as 'The Mall of America in the USA even has its own amusement park with four roller coasters for shoppers to ride in.' on page 11).

Word meaning and spelling

- Final /er/ spelling pattern – 'shopper', 'roller', 'flower', 'over', 'burger'.
- Longer words require breaking into syllables: 'department', 'escalator', 'amusement'.

Curriculum links

Language Development – A role play corner could be designed as a few of the different types of shops in a shopping mall. The display and counter will be designed to support the type of service available in each shop. Props, dressing up clothes and environmental print would support role play of a range of different customer/shopkeeper dialogues.

Geography – Create floor plans for some shops and shopping malls in the locality. This work could be linked to mathematics investigations of linear measurement, either standard or arbitrary measures, whichever is appropriate for the age of the children.

ORANGE BAND

Title: Town Underground
Author: Jonathan Emmett

Genre: Non-fiction
Word count: 310

Overview

This non-fiction report presents some ways of living and working underground. Children can explore a range of different underground habitations and consider the reasons why people would choose to live underground. Photographs provide a view of the many ways to live and work underground.

For some young children, the idea of people living underground will be an unusual one. Teachers may need to support this with other information texts, and by making links with other more familiar concepts such as animals living underground. Non-fiction conventions are followed making this a useful text on which to demonstrate the features of report writing.

Learning outcomes

Children can:

- use a variety of non-fiction page layouts
- problem-solve longer words by breaking them apart using familiar syllables
- consider events and provide reasons for why they might have happened.

Developing reading comprehension

- The non-fiction layout gives lots of opportunities to check information in the text with illustrations, and comment on the text meaning.
- Consider why people might live underground: what might be the benefits and the drawbacks to living in underground towns?

Grammar and sentence structure

- Sentence structures are more formal and complex (for example, *'Some of the oldest underground places were temples that were cut out of rock.'* on page 12).
- Some sentences demonstrate causality (such as: *'so that people would remember him after he died.'* on page 14; *'in case there was a war'* on page 17).

Word meaning and spelling

- Unfamiliar terms and vocabulary specific to the topic (*'entrance'*, *'mined'*, *'caves'*).
- Longer words require breaking into syllables (*'underground'*, *'Rameses'*, *'unusual'*).

Curriculum links

Geography – Children could develop mapping skills by drawing a plan of a home underground. This could be based on a home in the text, or a home they would like to live in.

Science and Nature – In this text, we see some animals that make their homes underground. They all have different reasons for doing so. Children could use the Internet to explore why the animals named in the text – rabbits, foxes, bears and bats – choose to make their homes underground. Can they find any other animals that create burrows underground, or live in caves?

TURQUOISE BAND

Title: Power Cut
Author: Peter Millett

Genre: Fiction
Word count: 520

Overview

This story is about the Chen family: Mum, Dad, Amy and Ben. They are getting ready for their evening at home when there is a power cut. How they cope in the dark without any light or power, especially when the batteries in Dad's torch run out, is the subject of this story. The book is written in four short chapters to support sustained reading. Many children will have experienced a power cut, but it is important to establish their prior knowledge before reading this book with them.

Learning outcomes

Children can:

- sustain meaning and comprehension over longer texts, summarising the key events
- note and use speech punctuation paying attention to reporting clauses to aid expressive, fluent reading
- read more complex words using appropriate strategies including known phonic knowledge and syllabification.

Developing reading comprehension

- The story evolves over a series of connected episodes. Children can be encouraged to summarise the story, picking out the key events.
- Children will need to make inferential links between sentences to uphold meaning; for example, Amy's idea (page 16) is not directly explained and the reader needs to make the causal link here to the use of Amy's tablet as a source of light.

Grammar and sentence structure

- The story is told predominantly through dialogue, demarcated by speech marks.
- Sentences are varied for effect, for example by using shorter sentences ('*I can fix that problem.*') or by adding adverbial words and phrases ('*just then*', '*luckily*').

Word meaning and spelling

- Syllabification of longer words enables word study for spelling inflectional endings and words with suffixes.
- Verbs used in reporting clauses ('*groaned*', '*asked*') demonstrate character and support expressive reading.

Curriculum links

Science and Nature – This book will lead to lots of science experiments! Children could investigate with different torches and look at how far the beam will shine, or how long the battery will last. Try making shadow puppets, or drawing silhouettes by projecting a project a beam of light onto large sheets of paper. Experiment with melting ice: how long will it take to melt if there is no power to the freezer?

PSHE – The Chens had to find a way to get by without electricity for a few hours. Explore things in the home or in school that use electricity to run. What would they have to do if there was a power cut? How might they prepare? How would they help others?

TURQUOISE BAND

Title: Sang Kancil and the Tiger
Author: Jim Carrington

Genre: Fiction
Word count: 569

Overview

This is a retelling of a traditional tale about the little mouse deer, Sang Kancil. In this story, Sang Kancil meets a hungry tiger in the jungle. The tiger wants to eat the mouse deer. Told through a sequence of events and with a repetitive structure, Sang Kancil is able to demonstrate his wit and cunning to trick the tiger and avoid being eaten.

The children may previously have read 'Sang Kancil and the Crocodile' (Orange band). This will enable them to predict story style, linguistic features and expectations based on their knowledge of the main character.

Learning outcomes

Children can:

- gain understanding from the text with less reliance on picture cues
- use punctuation to read aloud with a greater expression
- read longer sentence structures to support comprehension
- tackle unfamiliar words that are not completely decodable, using a range of cue sources.

Developing reading comprehension

- Scope for inferential reading is provided in the tiger's acceptance of Sang Kancil's rather outlandish explanations.
- Connective inferences are required: why did Tiger bare his sharp teeth (page 5)? Why did he jump in the river when the bees were chasing him (page 11)?

Grammar and sentence structure

- Repetition of a range of simple and complex range of sentence structures for impact and effect.
- Dialogue between the two main characters is used to move the story forward.

Word meaning and spelling

- More literary-style phrasing is used (for example, 'Greedy thoughts filled Tiger's mind' on page 5).
- Characters are described by key vocabulary and word choice rather than directly (e.g. 'his sly smile' on page 4, 'bared his sharp teeth' on page 5).

Curriculum links

Science and Nature – Find out more about tigers from non-fiction texts and the Internet. Particularly, explore their habitat and eating habits. How realistic is the story of Sang Kancil and the Tiger?

Literacy – Read other traditional tales of cunning tricks from a range of different cultures. Compare animal traits and ways in which they are portrayed.

TURQUOISE BAND

Title: Sinbad Goes to Sea
Author: Ian Whybrow

Genre: Fiction
Word count: 361

Overview

This story is a simple retelling of the first of the Seven Voyages of Sinbad. In this story Sinbad is poor so he seeks his fortune by going to sea on an adventure with some sailors. On the voyage, they find an island, but all is not what it seems. The story develops over a series of events, with Sinbad returning home rich from his adventure.

This book is written in the style of a traditional story, and provides a high-interest focus for children interested in adventure and excitement. Sinbad's adventures continue with 'Sinbad and the Roc' (Purple band).

Learning outcomes

Children can:

- read more complex multi-syllabic words, recognising known chunks and using phonic skills
- sustain reading through longer sentence structures of more than one clause
- monitor how their reading is sounding, checking that they understand what is read and self-correcting where necessary.

Developing reading comprehension

- A strong story plot enables children to consider cause and effect.
- Familiarity with the language and format of traditional stories supports comprehension.

Grammar and sentence structure

- Use of simple connectives ('and', 'but', 'so') to join clauses.
- Use of literary phrasing for effect and impact, for example: 'The sailors were happy, but Sinbad was not!' on page 6.

Word meaning and spelling

- Regular past tense verbs are used to describe action and motive.
- Spelling of compound words from known parts of words ('somewhere', 'something').

Curriculum links

Science and Nature – Sinbad and the sailors land on a whale. Find out about real-life whales in non-fiction texts and on the Internet.

Geography – The boat Sinbad sails on is going to the Land of Ice and Snow. What would this land be like? Why might the sailors be going there? Who would live there? Children can create this unknown land, using resource texts to consider what the landscape features would look like.

TURQUOISE BAND

**Title: The Great Jewelled Egg Mystery
(Benchmark Text)
Author: Gabby Pritchard**

Genre: Fiction
Word count: 435

Overview

One day, three children, Nadim, Farid and Aisha, go to the shopping mall with their father. Aisha loves mystery stories and would like to be a detective. The children go to listen to a mystery story in the book shop. Afterwards, as they are sitting waiting for Dad, they find a beautiful jewelled egg which has been left by the seat. They set out to trace its owner. The story builds over a series of elaborated events. Eventually, the children are able to return the egg and its mechanical singing bird to its rightful owner.

Learning outcomes

Children can:

- gain meaning from the text with less reliance on illustrations, checking and self correcting to ensure comprehension
- notice punctuation and use this to read with expression
- sustain reading through longer sentence structures and over a series of events
- read more complex words using a range of strategies.

Developing reading comprehension

- Characterisation and plotline provide strong support for the necessary inferential reading skills required.
- The title calls this book a mystery. What do the children understand this to mean? What are the features that make this a mystery story?
- The plot occurs over time, indicated by temporal connectives to demonstrate the sequence (such as *'as they left the book shop'* on page 3).

Grammar and sentence structure

- Dialogue is interspersed with narrative in telling the story.
- Punctuation is used to support phrased fluent reading, and to aid comprehension.

Word meaning and spelling

- Adjectival words (*'sadly'*) and phrases (*'through the crowd'*) to convey meaning and intent.
- Reporting clauses use a variety of verbs (*'laughed'*, *'replied'*, *'cried'*).

Curriculum links

Geography – The children use a map to locate possible places the egg may have come from. Look at other maps and diagrams of locales with which children are familiar. Plan routes from one place to another.

Literacy – Read and write mystery stories. What are the elements needed to make a mystery tale work well?

TURQUOISE BAND

Title: How Chocolate is Made
Author: Claire Llewellyn

Genre: Non-fiction
Word count: 505

Overview

This non-fiction text is predominantly an explanation text, demonstrating how chocolate is made. Beginning with where the beans are grown and harvested through to the many ways that chocolate is used, the step-by-step process is outlined. Additionally, a simple procedural text is included so children can make their own chocolate product.

Unlike some other types of non-fiction, explanation texts are generally read chronologically as they follow a sequence of events. Key structural non-fiction features to support the reading of information are represented, including maps, diagrams and 'Did you know?' boxes.

Learning outcomes

Children can:

- locate information in the text which supports comprehension
- understand and use charts, labels, and instructions
- problem-solve new topic words that are not completely decodable.

Developing reading comprehension

- The sequence is important in explanation texts. Can children orally retell or write the process of making chocolate, using the book to confirm their decisions?
- Non-fiction features such as labels, captions, diagrams and headings are used effectively to support meaning and to add information.
- Children are encouraged to note words that they do not understand, predicting from the context in the text and checking in the glossary.

Grammar and sentence structure

- Sentences follow the language features of the genre style (for example, imperative verbs for instructions; present tense for explanation).
- Different punctuation styles are used for labels and captions.

Word meaning and spelling

- Time connectives ('*then*', '*after*', '*next*').
- Reading and spelling topic words, using the glossary to find out their meaning.

Curriculum links

Science and Nature – Children could experiment with melting and cooling chocolate in different ways, and at different temperatures.

Maths – Create other pie charts to represent aspects familiar to the children (for example, the number of siblings each child has, or different modes of transport coming to school).

TURQUOISE BAND

Title: Draw the World
Author: Catherine Chambers

Genre: Non-fiction
Word count: 491

Overview

This attractive non-fiction book combines report with instruction for a mixed-genre approach. Different patterns and pictures from around the world are described. Then readers are offered the opportunity to draw the patterns for themselves.

The book's approach allows children to consolidate non-fiction reading skills encountered in earlier bands of *Cambridge Reading Adventures*: see, for example 'How Cars are Made' at Blue band, and 'Baking Bread' at Green band. The activities described are easily accessible for the young reader, and support the development of reading for information skills.

Learning outcomes

Children can:

- recognise key structural features of the genres represented
- use non-fiction text features (contents, glossary, index, maps) effectively
- read unfamiliar words that are not completely decodable, using a range of cue sources.

Developing reading comprehension

- A mixed genre approach provides a range of text features and sentence structures suitable to support the development of more advanced reading comprehension at Turquoise band.
- Clear sequenced steps enable the reader to locate specific information and to follow the instructions.

Grammar and sentence structure

- Longer, more formal sentences to convey ideas.
- Sentences are longer and contain more information, often with the use of commas in lists.

Word meaning and spelling

- Topic and specialist words are defined in the glossary.
- Verbs are used appropriately in each genre (imperative verbs for instructional texts).

Curriculum links

Art – Explore the activities suggested. Collect more examples of art from around the world from books and websites. Find out more about the legends depicted in art, such as the Dreamtime in Aboriginal drawings.

Maths – Explore symmetry through geometric patterning. Children could draw a small regular pattern of their own and then write instructions for a friend to follow to see if it can be reproduced accurately.

TURQUOISE BAND

Title: Motorcycles
Author: Andy Belcher

Genre: Non-fiction
Word count: 655

Overview

A non-fiction report, this text explores the development of motorcycles from the earliest types to those of the present day, and details some of their more important aspects. Readers learn about the design features of motorcycles, and the safety measures riders need to take. It explores different types of motorcycles from around the world, including some the children will be familiar with from their own setting.

Teachers will be able to make links with other non-chronological report texts in *Cambridge Reading Adventures*, such as 'Super Malls' and 'Life on the Reef' at Orange band.

Learning outcomes

Children can:

- locate information in the text which supports their comprehension
- use labelled diagrams to develop understanding
- problem-solve new topic words that are not completely decodable.

Developing reading comprehension

- Many specific and technical terms are used. Teachers will need to provide a thorough introduction, covering the important terms and technical parts of the motorcycle, before children read this book independently.
- Labelled diagrams provide clear graphics to support learning how to read for information effectively.

Grammar and sentence structure

- Sentences follow the language features of the genre style (for example, present tense, language structures showing the focus on generic groups, for example, '*Motorcycles have ...*'; '*Motorcycles can ...*').
- Different punctuation styles used for labels and captions.
- Text is grouped into topics, typical in a non-chronological report.

Word meaning and spelling

- Decoding multisyllabic technical terms that are likely to be novel to the young reader ('*chopper*', '*sidecar*', '*tarmac*', '*motocross*', '*mechanics*').
- Reading and spelling topic words, using the glossary to find out their meaning.

Curriculum links

Science and Nature - Children could label other transport and riders/drivers in the same style as pages 6 and 20.

History - Discuss other modes of transport, comparing early versions and contemporary versions (bicycles, buses and aeroplanes, for example). Support the discussion with photographs. This could lead to writing activities to draw comparisons between the two examples.

TURQUOISE BAND

Title: Clever Computers
Author: Jonathan Emmett

Genre: Non-Fiction
Word count: 363

Overview

Almost all children will have had experience with computers, both at home and in school. This non-fiction text, part historical recount and part non-chronological report, details the growth and development of computer technology. Early computers were little more than calculators. The book introduces early inventors such as Charles Babbage, whose work provided early prototypes of the computers we use today.

Learning outcomes

Children can:

- read a range of genres, recognising and using key structural features
- explain and use headings, labels, captions and glossaries
- employ appropriate strategies to read new or unfamiliar words.

Developing reading comprehension

- Some children may not link the word '*computer*' to tablets or mobile phones. Establish that these, too, are computers.
- Page 2 tells the reader: '*Computers are machines that can think!*' What do the children understand by this? Do computers really think? Use this to explore the things computers can do for us.
- Text features, such as labels, captions, content and index pages, support the young reader in searching for and locating information.

Grammar and sentence structure

- Sentence features are appropriate to genre style: past tense verbs and time connectives ('*then*', '*now*') to support recount; present tense and generic participants ('*people*', '*computers*') for report.
- Longer, more complex sentences, including subordinate clauses, supported by punctuation.
- Use of ellipses to demonstrate continuation of a sentence across the page.

Word meaning and spelling

- Reading and spelling subject-specific vocabulary, supported by context and glossary.
- Use of comparatives ('*bigger*', '*smaller*', '*cheaper*'), particular in exploring the spelling convention to double the consonant of CVC words when adding the morpheme '*er*'.

Curriculum links

Science and Nature – Investigate how many different types of computers are used around the school and at home, and for what purposes.

Maths – The Enigma machine was used to crack codes. Children could set simple codes for their friends to solve – such as substituting each letter of the alphabet with a number or sum of numbers, or reversing the order of the alphabet (A becomes Z, B becomes Y, and so on).

PURPLE BAND

Title: Sandstorm!
Author: Peter Millett

Genre: Fiction
Word count: 631

Overview

Shan and Jia are out riding with their Mum and Dad. Frustrated at the slow pace of their ride, the two children ask if they can ride on ahead, but they soon lose sight of their parents as they become caught in a ferocious sandstorm. The children stay calm, and Shan's quick thinking keeps them and their ponies safe during the storm. This exciting adventure story builds tension over a sequence of time and towards a resolution. When Mum and Dad find them, Shan and Jia decide to take the slow and steady way home after all. The book is written in short chapters to support sustained reading.

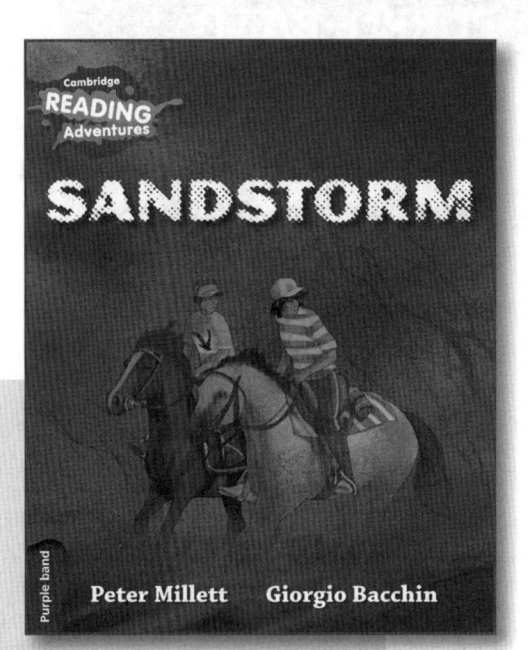

Learning outcomes

Children can:

- identify and describe characters
- read silently or quietly at a more rapid pace
- take note of punctuation and use it to keep track of longer sentences
- solve most unfamiliar words using appropriate word-reading strategies.

Developing reading comprehension

- The text provides opportunity to consider characterisation and motive, and the implications of action.
- The familiar theme of being lost is viewed through an unusual setting, giving scope for children to relate the novel context to their own experiences.
- Shan's quick thinking saves both him and sister from the worst of the storm. Consider the actions he took, and why (e.g. on pages 8 and 9).

Grammar and sentence structure

- Sentences are longer and more complex, using a range of causal connectives to sustain more than one idea.
- Variation in sentence structure for dramatic effect (e.g. page 20).

Word meaning and spelling

- Vocabulary choices to demonstrate heightened tension and change of mood (e.g. 'grinned' 'gasped' 'frowned').
- The spelling of past tense 'ed' verbs, exploring conventions for doubling consonants (e.g. 'hugged', 'grinned') and 'y' to 'ied' (such as 'replied').

Curriculum links

Geography – Work on climatic conditions in desert regions. Compare with other weather phenomena such as snowstorms, tornados, etc.

PSHE – The theme of staying safe is explored. Children could write warning posters or safety leaflets, particularly related to risks in their own context.

PURPLE BAND

Title: Sinbad and the Giant Roc
Author: Ian Whybrow

Genre: Fiction
Word count: 586

Overview

This is a retelling of the second of the seven voyages of Sinbad. Sinbad is off on another adventure. This time he meets a giant bird called a Roc. It will be helpful if the children have already read the first voyage 'Sinbad Goes to Sea' earlier in *Cambridge Reading Adventures* (Turquoise band). A series of events build over time to a resolution, which is left open ready for Sinbad's next adventure.

Learning outcomes

Children can:

- read at a faster pace, sometimes silently
- compare the story features with those of other traditional tales
- use the language of time to discuss story sequence
- solve new, unfamiliar words using appropriate reading strategies.

Developing reading comprehension

- The character of Sinbad is developed through his behaviour, dialogue and action.
- Children seek and locate evidence in text to demonstrate their understanding.

Grammar and sentence structure

- Adverbial phases signal the passing of time ('*At first*; '*But soon*').
- Sentence structure is varied for literary effect, for example: '*He could see sticks – lots of sticks.*' (page 10).

Word meaning and spelling

- Language structures follow elements of traditional retellings, such as the use of '*Once Upon a Time*' to open the story, and in vocabulary choices: '*to faraway lands*' (page 4).
- Some novel, context-specific vocabulary is introduced, such as '*merchants*' and '*treasure*' for which children will need to use effective word reading strategies including breaking words into known chunks.

Curriculum links

Science and Nature – A Roc is a mythical creature but it has the features of a bird of prey. Children could use non-fiction texts and information on websites to find out about real birds of prey and write their own non-fiction reports. They could innovate on the genre to create imaginary reports about Rocs.

Art – The illustrator has drawn his interpretation of what he thinks a Roc may look like. Ask the children to draw or paint their idea of a Roc referring to photographs of birds of prey, or pictures of other mythical creatures for support.

PURPLE BAND

Title: King Fox (Benchmark Text)
Author: Tom Bradman

Genre: Fiction
Word count: 636

Overview

Fox wakes up late one morning, feeling hungry. He goes out to get some breakfast, but none of the other animals will help him – they are all too busy hiding from Tiger. While Fox puzzles about what to do, Tiger looms up behind him – now it looks like Fox will be Tiger's breakfast! Fox runs away as fast as he can. He encounters some foresters and their master in the forest. Watching them gives Fox an idea. In a cunning plan, Fox finds a way to outwit Tiger and get his breakfast at the same time.

Learning outcomes

Children can:

- discuss story setting and compare with similar traditional tales
- draw together ideas and information from across a whole text
- identify and describe characters
- solve most unfamiliar words on-the-run by blending.

Developing reading comprehension

- There are complicated layers of meaning and the book offers a high level of challenge to support comprehension.
- This story provides opportunity for inference beyond the text, such asking why Fox pretends to be the king of the forest and why Tiger believes him. Are the animals really frightened of Fox?

Grammar and sentence structure

- The use of dialogue and adverbial phrases serve to indicate how Fox might be saying one thing whilst thinking another. This is an important literary grammar technique which supports comprehension (see page 18).
- The choice of verbs illustrates characterisation (for example, when Fox orders Tiger to follow him, on page 20).

Word meaning and spelling

There are several naturally occurring uses of the /ow/ grapheme. The text provides opportunity to support effective blending through a word to read unfamiliar words and to explore alternative vowel diagraph choices.

In the guided reading lesson, children can explore new words and effective word choice, and consider how this helps to convey the meaning of the story (e.g. '*bellowed*', '*snarled*', '*terrified*').

Curriculum links

Citizenship – There is potential to relate to children's own experiences of respect and authority, and the text can support discussions about leadership and courage.

PURPLE BAND

Title: Going on a Plane
Author: Alison Sage

Genre: Non-fiction
Word count: 686

Overview

Millions of people travel by plane. In this book, children find out what happens at the airport and on the plane. Plane travel may well be something with which the children are familiar. This book offers the opportunity to revisit some of the things they will have experienced, or to introduce plane travel to children who have yet to do so. Written predominantly as a report, the text offers some chronology in the sequencing of events, more in keeping with explanatory texts, which offers a degree of challenge at Purple band.

Learning outcomes

Children can:

- use non-fiction features to support understanding of the text
- adapt to the language of non-fiction texts, using the language structures and grammatical conventions of the genre
- attempt unfamiliar words, using known syllable chunks, monitoring that their meaning is understood.

Developing reading comprehension

- Non-fiction text features such as captions, labels and facts boxes support comprehension.
- Establishing prior knowledge and experience supports understanding of new or unfamiliar concepts.

Grammar and sentence structure

- Language structures and verb tenses are in keeping with the genre, for example: generic features of report-writing ('*passengers*', '*some airports*'); chronology of explanation ('*When the plane is in the air ...*', '*soon the plane lands ...*').
- Longer, more complex sentences, including the use of connectives to join clauses ('*The flight attendant says goodbye to the passengers as they leave the plane.*' on page 21).

Word meaning and spelling

- Reading of new or unfamiliar multi-syllabic words ('*conveyor*', '*departure*') using the context and glossary to ensure the meaning is understood.
- Spelling of present tense verb endings ('*says*', '*tells*', '*brings*') and the use of auxiliary verbs ('*everyone is waiting*', '*passengers are boarding*', '*we will be landing*'), noting the spelling of the /ing/ inflection on the main verb.

Curriculum links

Geography – Use a map to chart where in the world the children have travelled.

Science and Nature – Children could experiment with different designs of paper planes. What is the best paper to use? What helps the planes to fly further or to stay in the air longest?

PURPLE BAND

Title: Ships, Boats and Things that Float
Author: Scoular Anderson

Genre: Non-fiction
Word count: 858

Overview

Throughout history, people have devised many different ways to travel on water. In this brightly coloured, illustrated text, written in the non-chronological report genre, children can find out lots of interesting facts about how people learned to travel around the world in boats and ships. This book is a companion text to 'Sticks, Bricks and Bits of Stone' (White band) which comes later in *Cambridge Reading Adventures*. The usual non-fiction features, such as labels and captions, are used in an entertaining way to add meaning and support comprehension.

Learning outcomes

Children can:

- recognise how words are used to literary effect to achieve authorial purpose
- adapt to the different styles employed in the text
- take note of punctuation and use it to keep track of longer sentences
- solve most unfamiliar words using appropriate word-reading strategies, and monitor that meaning is gained.

Developing reading comprehension

- Children can select areas of personal interest to research, learning how to pose questions and locate information in the text to provide the answer.
- There are some examples of literary language that are unusual usage in non-chronological reports (such as the heading '*Quicker by Boat*' on page 2). Teachers will need to support children in ensuring these are understood.
- Children should seek clarification when they are unsure of word meaning, making effectively use of the glossary and confirming their understanding by rereading the word in context.

Grammar and sentence structure

- Sentences incorporate a range of connectives to develop ideas over two or more clauses.
- Verb usage is more advanced, including use of conditional verbs.

Word meaning and spelling

- Subject-specific words, supported by glossary and labelling.
- Longer, multi-syllabic words ('*container*', '*nowadays*') requiring attention to word detail.

Curriculum links

Geography – not all children live in regions served by the sea. Topics could explore modes of transport in land-locked countries.

History – use this book in conjunction with other non-fiction texts to investigate the development of transport and travel, or if studying specific periods of history such as the Ancient Egyptians.

PURPLE BAND

Title: Pterosaur!
Author: Jon Hughes

Genre: Non-fiction
Word count: 503

Overview

What were pterosaurs? Where did they live and when? This non-fiction report gives the reader the opportunity to find out about what pterosaurs were, what they looked like and how we know about them. We learn about different types of pterosaurs: those which were meat eaters and were big enough to hunt dinosaurs; others which were smaller and ate insects. Readers can also find out about how we know so much about pterosaurs today, even though they died out millions of years ago. The headings support the text by drawing information in to clear themes. Specialised vocabulary is defined in a glossary. A contents page allows the reader to search for specific information.

Learning outcomes

Children can:

- solve most unfamiliar words
- pose questions, and record these in writing, prior to reading non-fiction, to find answers
- locate parts of the text that give particular information and use this information in discussion
- use language of time to express that pterosaurs lived many millions of years ago, before mankind and animals that are living now.

Developing reading comprehension

- Additional information is provided in the facts boxes.
- Teachers can support the reading of non-fiction for information by modelling questioning strategies and formulating answers based on information located in the text.

Grammar and sentence structure

- The past tense is used throughout.
- Sentences are complex (e.g. 'Pterosaurs often lived in large groups, like seabirds do today').

Word meaning and spelling

- There is opportunity to reinforce word-reading skills on unfamiliar words and technical vocabulary.
- The glossary, captions and contents can be used to monitor understanding and develop vocabulary.

Curriculum links

Science and Nature – Read other reports about dinosaurs and pterosaurs in order to compare and contrast how information is conveyed in different texts.

Mathematics – The text gives some information about size. Gather information about the dimensions of dinosaurs and order them from the smallest to the biggest. This could be extended by providing measurements for present day animals in order to begin to develop a concept of relative size.

PURPLE BAND

Title: The Book of World Facts
Author: Anita Ganeri

Genre: Non-fiction
Word count: 622

Overview

Written predominantly in a report genre, this compendium brings together interesting geographical facts, arranged thematically, that will be of interest to children wherever they live.

The book offers many useful links to other areas of the curriculum and opportunity to explore specific areas of interest. A range of non-fiction text features support the reader to access information. There are some more unusual features for this type of non-fiction text, such as the inclusion of cartoon illustrations. This provides a suitable challenge for readers at Purple band.

Learning outcomes

Children can:

- recognise how specific language is used to present information in non-fiction texts
- take note of punctuation, using it to keep track of longer sentences and noting impact
- attempt unfamiliar words, including those not completely decodable, monitoring that their meaning is understood.

Developing reading comprehension

- A mix of photographs, illustrations, maps and charts serve to provide information.
- This book is a good starting point for children to identify areas of interest, leading to more in-depth study.

Grammar and sentence structure

- Longer, more complex sentences incorporate adjectives and adverbial phrases.
- Captions and labels are punctuated correctly according to purpose.

Word meaning and spelling

- Spelling of comparative and superlative adjectives ('*saltier*', '*highest*'), exploring changes to the root words (for example, doubling the consonant when writing '*biggest*').
- Reading of novel or unfamiliar, multi-syllabic words ('*population*'; '*Antarctica*') and ensuring these are understood through use of the context and the glossary.

Curriculum links

Geography – Use the sections of the book to introduce more in-depth study of particular areas of interest, such as work on rainforests.

Literacy – The short sections detailing each World Fact could become the basis for report writing, comparing and contrasting the layout, grammar and style of other reports on the same subject.

GOLD BAND

Title: Tefo and the Lucky Football Boots
Author: Lauri Kubuitsile

Genre: Fiction
Word count: 974

Overview

This is another story in the series about Omar and his friends from the International School strand of *Cambridge Reading Adventures*. Children who have read the earlier stories previously (such as 'Omar Can Help', or 'Omar in Trouble') will be familiar with the characters and settings. The main character this time is Tefo.

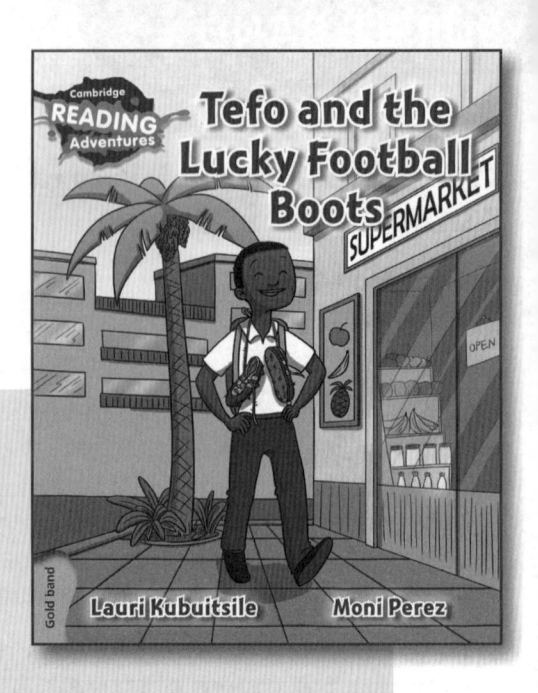

Tefo wants to play in the football team. But he is worried he is not good enough. He goes to Grandpa for help. Grandpa was once a famous footballer who had scored many goals for his team. He lends Tefo his old football boots, telling Tefo they are lucky. Tefo plays in the team and scores the winning goal. But one day Mum throws the old boots away. What will Tefo do now?

Learning outcomes

Children can:

- read through longer passages of text in paragraphs, sustaining meaning as they read
- monitor their own reading for accuracy and comprehension
- read more complex words using known vocabulary.

Developing reading comprehension

- There are time shifts in the story which add to the complexity of comprehension required. These are supported well by the illustrations.
- The storyline offers opportunity for discussion around confidence and self-belief: were the boots really 'lucky'? What was Grandpa's motivation for telling Tefo they were?
- The book is organised in five short chapters to support sustained reading at this band.

Grammar and sentence structure

- Time connectives portray the events over time.
- A range of simple and complex sentence structures used for impact and effect.
- Paragraphing supports organisation of ideas.

Word meaning and spelling

- Literary-style devices, such as sound effects (e.g. 'whoosh' on page 12,) and phrases (e.g. *Faster and faster he went* on page 9) are evident.
- Longer, more complex words (e.g. *everywhere*, *without*) are read using syllabification and known reading vocabulary.

Curriculum links

Social Science – Children could explore their own family history, and find out about what their grandparents did when they were younger.

Literacy – What are the children's aspirations for what they want to be when they grow up?

GOLD BAND

Title: Yu and the Great Flood
Author: Tony Bradman

Genre: Fiction
Word count: 696

Overview

Yu is good at solving problems. But can he beat Gong Gong the water monster? This adaptation of a well-known Chinese tale charts the triumph of good over evil. In this story a water monster called Gong Gong likes to make mischief. He sends a great flood which covers all the land of China. The emperor sends for Yu and orders him to stop the flood. Yu enlists the help of his friends, Yellow Dragon and Black Turtle. Together, they devise a plan to dig ditches to drain the water away. This enrages Gong Gong and a mighty battle ensues. Yu and his friends win the day, and the emperor is so pleased that he names Yu as his son and heir.

Learning outcomes

Children can:

- read fluently with attention to punctuation
- discuss and interpret character
- solve new words using print detail while attending to meaning and syntax.

Developing reading comprehension

- The story gives hints as to character motivation: why is Gong Gong set on flooding the land? What do we know already of Yu before the story starts? How does his character develop throughout the story?
- Yu has to think quickly during the battle to defeat Gong Gong. Children can consider the implications of his decisions and offer alternative solutions to the problem.

Grammar and sentence structure

- Sentences are longer and more complex.
- The vocabulary implies the feelings of the author.
- Variation in sentence structure for dramatic effect (e.g. page 9).

Word meaning and spelling

- Vocabulary choices to demonstrate heightened tension and change of mood (e.g. 'roared' 'cheered' 'yelled').
- Literary effects used to build tension (e.g. use of ellipsis on page 13 and 18).

Curriculum links

Geography - Research techniques used to prevent floods in different regions of the world (e.g. use of vegetation, drainage, barriers, dams, reservoirs, dykes, etc).

Science and Nature - Explore water displacement through some simple activities. For example, half fill a container with a wide opening. Half fill with water and mark the level with a pen. Then, using small pebbles, coins and marbles in turn, investigate how far the water rises if three are added, then five, then ten. Mark each result with a pen.

GOLD BAND

Title: Lost at Sea (Benchmark Text)
Author: Peter Millett

Genre: Fiction
Word count: 564

Overview

Adeline and her father are lost at sea. Written in three short chapters, this story follows the events as they seek rescue from their small life raft after an accident at sea. Will they be rescued in time? The plot provides tension which keeps children engaged over this longer text at Gold band.

Learning outcomes

Children can:

- note literary effects used by writers, using these to aid comprehension and expression
- consider vocabulary choice and evaluate its effectiveness in achieving authorial intent
- use a widening range of punctuation to support understanding across longer sentences.

Developing reading comprehension

- The longer story line supports character development.
- The events leading to the accident are mentioned briefly but not elaborated upon, providing opportunity to develop discussion and inferential skills.

Grammar and sentence structure

- Longer, more complex sentences require the reader to take note of punctuation, for example *'When Adeline awoke the next morning, she was cold and hungry.'* (page 12).
- Sentences vary in length and structure for impact and effect: *'Oh no, this is bad. Really bad.'* (page 10).
- Speech and dialogue inform the reader of the story action: *'It's a ship! Have they seen us?'* (page 13).

Word meaning and spelling

- Word choice in reporting clauses convey character thought and intention: (*'cried'*, *'gasped'*, *'sighed'*).
- Conventions for spelling past tense verbs such as doubling the consonant (*'grinned'*) or changing /y/ to /ied/ (*'worried'*).

Curriculum links

History – Read true stories of sea rescues, using non-fiction books and internet sources. You could also make a link with fiction, such as 'Robinson Crusoe'.

Science and Nature – Adeline makes her tin foil into a mirror to signal the ship. Would this really work? Try this out with the children. What else would do the same job?

GOLD BAND

Title: Animals of the Ice Age
Author: Jon Hughes

Genre: Non-fiction
Word count: 904

Overview

This non-fiction report text explores how animals of the Ice Age lived, and why they became extinct. The climatic changes that bring about an ice age are considered. The text explores how some animals survived an ice age whilst others perished in the freezing conditions. The text then looks at specific animals of the Ice Age, such as woolly mammoths and sabre-toothed tigers in more detail, and discusses theories as to why such animals became extinct.

Non-fiction text features, such as sub-headings, fact boxes and diagrams, are included. Captions provide additional information to that given in the main body of the text. Specialised vocabulary is defined in a glossary. The index can be used to locate specific areas of interest. This book could be linked to other similar themed reports in *Cambridge Reading Adventures*, such as 'Pterosaurs!' (Purple band).

Learning outcomes

Children can:

- recognize alternative spellings to read longer and more complex words
- make full use of non-fiction layout
- locate and interpret information in non-fiction
- pose questions, and record these in writing, prior to reading non-fiction to find answers.

Developing reading comprehension

- There is much conjecture about what is actually known of these animals and why they died. The author displays this in the use of tentative language (e.g. *'probably lived off roots and berries'* on page 9) and avoiding direct statements (*'Scientists think ...'* on page 18).
- The text does not directly state why mammoths were woolly, but it is inferred through the reference to the cold conditions. This will support development of inferential skills.

Grammar and sentence structure

- Sentences are longer and more complex (e.g. *'We know about mammoths because we have found paintings of them in the caves where early humans lived.'*)
- Commas used to punctuate sentences with dependent (subordinate) clauses (e.g. *'If we could go back thousands of years to when the Earth was cooler, what might we see?'*).

Word meaning and spelling

- There is opportunity to reinforce word-reading skills on unfamiliar words and technical vocabulary.
- Understanding of new vocabulary is supported by the glossary and the non-fiction text features, such as labels and captions.

Curriculum links

Geography – Explore the topography of the region in which the children live for evidence of ice age features. How does this compare with regions that were not covered by ice during the Ice Age (flat deserts, rain forests).

Science and Nature – Read other reports about mammoths and other ice age mammals, to build on the information provided here.

GOLD BAND

Title: Scarface: the Real Lion King
Author: Jonathan and Angela Scott

Genre: Non-fiction
Word count: 825

Overview

This non-fiction text is a blend of recount and report writing. It follows the adventures of a young lion called Scarface as he sets out to establish a pride of his own. Using real-life photography, the book documents Scarface's adventures as, with his three friends, he seeks to take over the Marsh Lions' Pride from its two old leaders, Clawed and Romeo.

The text includes the features expected in non-fiction texts (fact boxes, labels, index). Technical terms associated with lions and other relevant information is explained in a glossary.

Learning outcomes

Children can:

- skim-read illustrations and sub-headings to speculate what the book might be about
- adapt to different text types with growing flexibility
- solve most unfamiliar words on-the-run by blending less common digraphs
- pose questions, and record these in writing, prior to reading non-fiction, to find answers
- locate parts of the text that give particular information.

Developing reading comprehension

- The title 'Lion King' is a reference to popular culture (the 1994 cartoon film of the same name). Children may not automatically make this interferential link and the teacher may need to explain.
- The reader is not told how Scarface got the scar which gave him his name. Children will need to infer this information, gleaning clues from the text, such as that Scarface was driven out of his original pride (page 7).

Grammar and sentence structure

- Sentences follow the grammatical expectations of recount and reports (e.g. past tense verbs in recount sections, and present tense in report sections).
- Complex sentences with two or more clauses support the development of comprehension.

Word meaning and spelling

- There is opportunity to reinforce word-reading skills on unfamiliar words and technical vocabulary.
- The glossary and other sources are used to monitor understanding and develop vocabulary.

Curriculum links

Science and Nature – Read reports about lions and other meat-eating mammals. Compare and contrast how the information is conveyed in different texts.

Conservation – Lions are now an endangered species. Use the Internet to find out more about the work of the wildlife rangers, and conservation projects which aim to protect lions in the wild.

Literacy – The book is called the 'Real Lion King'. Explore the reference to the popular book/film/musical. Write one of the events in the text from Scarface's point of view.

GOLD BAND

Title: Giants of the Ocean
Author: Catherine Bowley

Genre: Non-fiction
Word count: 1010

Overview

Whales are amazing and wonderful creatures. There are many different kinds of whale. This non-chronological report provides interesting information about whales: how they live and breathe, where they live and what they eat. Different species of whales are introduced. The text uses a range of non-fiction features, especially making effective use of facts boxes for information supplementary to that in the main body of the text. Specialised vocabulary is defined in a glossary. Additional background information is provided for the teacher.

The book was written and produced in association with ORCA, which is a UK-based whale and dolphin conservation charity dedicated to the long term protection of whales, dolphins and porpoises and their habitats.

Learning outcomes

Children can:

- read longer unfamiliar words using effective reading strategies, and can monitor their own understanding
- use a range of non-fiction features successfully to gain information from the text
- search for information to answer specific questions and to raise others.

Developing reading comprehension

- Page layout is varied as appropriate for purpose (see for example, pages 8 and 9). Children will need to recognise and understand how page layout and design support comprehension of text, or provide additional information.
- Subject-specific information is described (such as how baleen is used to filter the seafood the whale eats). Teachers will need to support children to clarify and explain this in their own words to demonstrate comprehension.

Grammar and sentence structure

- Sentences are longer, often with two or more clauses demarcated by commas (e.g. *'Baleen whales are big, but they eat some of the smallest creatures on Earth.'*).
- Inverted commas are used to show that a word is being used in a different meaning to that usually understood (e.g. *'talk'*, *'sing'* on page 10).

Word meaning and spelling

- Unfamiliar words and technical vocabulary provide opportunity for rehearsing word-reading skills, including use of syllabification.
- Understanding of new vocabulary is supported by the glossary and by text features such as labels and captions.

Curriculum links

Science and Nature – Whales are mammals. Use the book as a starting point to investigate characteristics of mammals in other non-fiction texts and on websites. Use the information gathered to write non-chronological reports about other mammals.

Social Studies – Explore the ORCA website and find out more about the conservation work carried out by this organisation.

GOLD BAND

Title: Rags to Bags
Author: Anita Ganeri

Genre: Non-fiction
Word count: 417

Overview

This text explores the issues of waste and recycling by looking at the enterprising people who turn discarded plastic bags into usable objects. The text interweaves text features from report, persuasion and explanation genres to fulfil its purpose. The introduction of persuasive text at Gold band is unusual and will need supporting. The title is abstract and will need to be explained to young readers.

Learning outcomes

Children can:

- scan the text to locate specific information
- read longer unfamiliar words by paying attention to component parts
- critically evaluate the information given in content and presentation.

Developing reading comprehension

- Non-fiction features, such as a glossary, index and facts boxes, enable children to practise and consolidate reading for information skills.
- The use of rhetorical questioning encourages readers to pose questions and think about answers whilst reading.

Grammar and sentence structure

- The grammatical structures reflect range and purpose: persuasive language addresses the reader directly ('*Have you ever wondered ...*'); the making of bags from recycled plastic uses explanation features such as time connectives ('*First rag-pickers collect the bags.*') to order sequence of events.
- Sentences are more complex, using commas to denote lists and to separate clauses.
- Questioning is used to engage the reader directly: '*What do you do with your bag when you get home?*'

Word meaning and spelling

- New or unfamiliar vocabulary is explained in the glossary, or expanded upon in the facts boxes.
- Compound words such as '*handbags*' and '*landfill*' can be compared with the use of hyphenated words '*rag-pickers*'.

Curriculum links

Science and Nature – Many materials can be recycled. Possibly the most commonly-recycled material is paper. Children can make their own recycled paper from old used papers in the classroom.

PSHE – Begin a recycling awareness campaign in your school. Children can create posters, using persuasive language and advertising techniques, to encourage classmates to be aware of waste, and to know which materials can be recycled.

WHITE BAND

Title: The Great Escape
Author: Peter Millett

Genre: Fiction
Word count: 770

Overview

In this story, it is the whales that make a great escape after becoming beached. The story deals with how Selma overcomes her personal fear of the water to help save the whales. 'The Silk Road' and 'Yu and the Great Flood' are examples of texts that also deal with overcoming adversity.

Learning outcomes

Children can:

- take more conscious account of literary effects used by writers
- solve most unfamiliar words on-the-run by blending less common digraphs and recognizing alternative spellings to read longer and more complex words
- read silently or quietly at a more rapid pace, taking note of punctuation and using it to keep track of longer sentences.

Developing reading comprehension

- Focusing on specific words and phrases and discussing how they influence the messages and meanings the reader gets will help develop reading comprehension at a higher level.

Grammar and sentence structure

- Amount of direct speech requiring use of punctuation to read fluently and with expression.
- Literary phrases; 'Out of the blue', 'as she watched whale after whale...'
- Adverbial phrases

Word meaning and spelling

- Challenging vocabulary; 'beached', 'aground', 'choppy', 'boomed'.
- Decoding polysyllabic words: 'horizon', 'distressed', 'directions'.
- Inflection – er; 'safe/safer', 'calm/calmer', 'big/bigger'.

Curriculum links

Science and Nature – Activities flowing from this text include: the harmful effects of the sun; the power of water; sea mammals. All of these topics could lead to research to write information books that could be shared as class texts.

PSHE – How we overcome things that we are frightened of could lead to some creative and reflective writing either on themselves or familiar story characters. For example, children's picture books, such as 'The Owl who was afraid of the Dark', 'Can't you sleep Little Bear', 'Curious George goes to the Hospital' and 'The Gruffalo' could be shared as starting points to creative writing.

Further reading in *Cambridge Reading Adventures* that links to the ocean include: 'Life on the Reef', 'Giants of the Ocean'.

WHITE BAND

Title: Mei and the Pirate Queen
Author: Tony Bradman

Genre: Fiction
Word count: 1219

Overview

Mei runs away from home and is captured by pirates. In a brave encounter, she confronts the Pirate Queen. Ultimately, good triumphs over bad. The story line is sustained over time and place, with a series of events culminating in a conclusion, but with an opening for further adventures. The subject matter can be challenging for some younger readers. In some regions, where modern-day piracy is an issue, teachers will need to handle the content of this story sensitively.

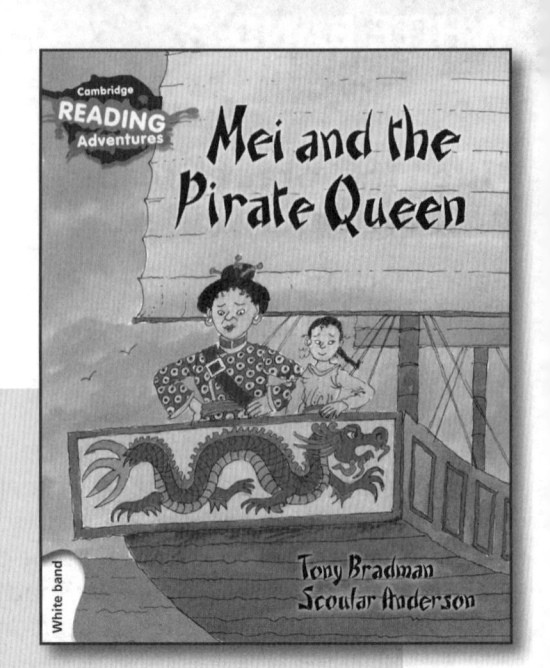

Learning outcomes

Children can:

- consider authorial intent in vocabulary choice and grammatical structure
- discuss personal interpretations, providing evidence from the text to support opinions
- read a wider range of new, unfamiliar words, relating these to known words and parts of words (such as suffixes and prefixes).

Developing reading comprehension

- Strong character description supports understanding of motive and action.
- Short chapters provide opportunity for summarising and predicting during the guided reading lesson.

Grammar and sentence structure

- Sentences are more complex, and grammatical structures are used to convey tension (such as the use of ellipsis on page 3).
- The use of connective words and adverbial phrases ('*A couple of days later*' and '*As the junk sailed on*') are used to structure the sequence of events.

Word meaning and spelling

- More sophisticated vocabulary choice serves to indicate action and motive: '*Suddenly, all the pirates looked nervous*', '*Everyone else just stared, open-mouthed*'.
- Adjectives and adjectival phrases ('*toughest*', '*nasty and cruel*', '*very unpleasant*') are used to describe character and mood.

Curriculum links

History – Use the Internet to investigate true stories of female pirates such as Anne Bonney, Sayyida al Hurra and Mary Read.

PSHE – Mei is brave and stands up to the Pirate Queen even though she is scared. Consider with the children times when they have been brave. They could read about other people in their specific context who have strived for human rights in the face of adversity.

WHITE BAND

Title: The Silk Road (Benchmark Text)
Author: Tony Bradman

Genre: Fiction
Word count: 1273

Overview

This is a story based on historical fact. After bandits destroy his home and kill his parents, Cheng has to leave his village and make his way alone in the world. No-one in the nearby villages will take him in, so he decides to join the merchants travelling on the Silk Road. Cheng works to earn his keep, and learns many new and interesting things. Travelling can be exciting but it can also be dangerous and lonely, too. One day, Cheng saves two of his fellow travellers from robbers. Cheng's kind heart and good deed lead to the two grateful travellers asking Cheng to travel with them: he had found a family and a home at last.

The sophisticated themes will be challenging for some younger, more able readers, but offer an opportunity for older, struggling readers to read a simpler text at a high interest level. This book is written in three chapters. It is possible to use the book over two guided reading lessons, setting Chapter 2 as an independent reading activity in between each lesson.

Learning outcomes

Children can:

- sustain interest in longer text, returning to it easily after a break
- explore how particular words and phrases are used
- express reasoned opinions about what is read
- monitor meaning and understanding, and take action when meaning is lost.

Developing reading comprehension

- The events unfold over three short chapters, requiring comprehension to be sustained over longer reading.
- Cheng is helped by many people along the way; but there are other people who do not help him. Use the story to discuss character motive.

Grammar and sentence structure

- Sentences are longer, with subordinate phrases or clauses.
- Paragraphing and page layout serve to support the meaning and build tension.
- The use of connective words and phrases (such as 'Eventually' and 'After a while') are used to structure the passing of time.

Word meaning and spelling

- New subject-specific vocabulary is introduced ('merchants', 'haggling').
- Meaning is monitored and checked through use of dictionaries and contextual information in text.
- Place names, titles and new vocabulary words are read using decoding and word-recognition skills.

Curriculum links

History – Read other accounts of the Silk Road in books or via the Internet.

Geography – Trace the route of the Silk Road on a modern map. Find what goods were traded from which countries along the route.

Citizenship – Cheng was lucky to meet with people who helped him along the way. Explore modern-day equivalent stories and biographies of people supporting others in times of trouble.

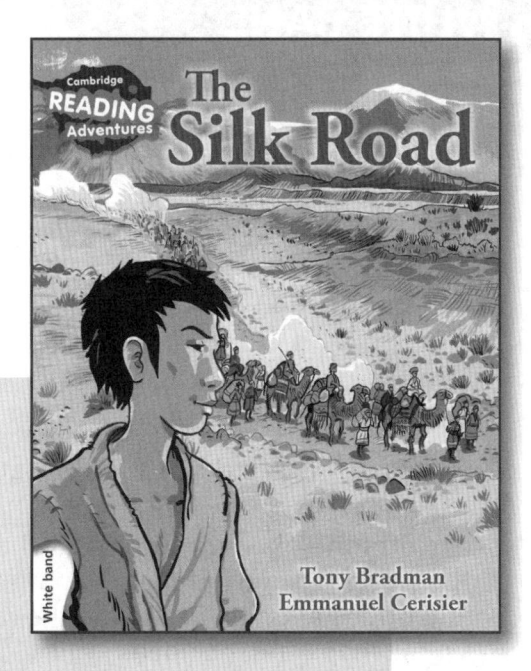

WHITE BAND

Title: Earthquakes
Author: Kathryn Harper

Genre: Non-fiction
Word count: 646

Overview

What is it really like in an earthquake? Why do earthquakes happen? This non-fiction report explores the phenomenon of earthquakes around the world. The technique of a narrator serves to add information and to guide the reader. Non-fiction features, such as diagrams and simple maps, are included.

Some children may never have experienced an earthquake. For others, the experience may be recent and all too real. This subject may need careful mediation in such instances.

Learning outcomes

Children can:

- read silently most of the time
- explain and evaluate use of the organizational features used to convey information
- draw together information from across the text to summarise what has been read
- express reasoned opinions about what is read, relating to own or others' experience.

Developing reading comprehension

- Children can evaluate the impact of the non-fiction devices (such as the 'talking expert') in conveying information effectively.
- Opportunities to predict what each section will be about, giving rationales for their predictions, such as clues in the headings (for example, 'be prepared') and confirming their predictions with evidence from the text.

Grammar and sentence structure

- Consider how particular words and phrases are used are for effect.
- Note how headings are used to summarise the content on each page.
- Complex sentences such as: 'Landslides can occur and fires can start if power cables and gas lines are broken.' (page 15) employ subordinate clauses to convey more than one idea.

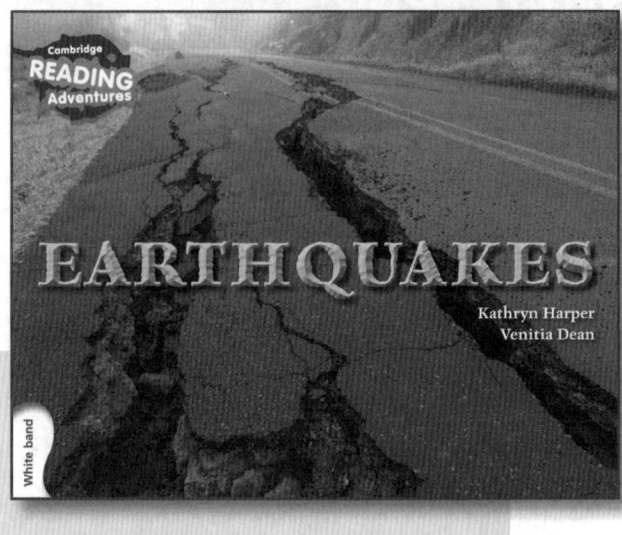

Word meaning and spelling

- Distinguish between the different styles used in the main text and the 'voice' of the scientific expert (for example, in providing additional information).
- Unfamiliar, technical words (such as 'tsunami' and 'tremor') are explained in the text and in the glossary.

Curriculum links

Geography – Look at websites and other non-fiction sources to explore regions mentioned in the text (such as San Francisco in the USA) and look at measures taken to prepare for earthquakes.

PSHE – For regions where an earthquake may have occurred recently, children could find ways to support the relief effort such as holding a school sale or through collecting clothing and bedding to send. Children can write posters to advertise events.

WHITE BAND

Title: Sticks and Bricks and Bits of Stone
Author: Scoular Anderson

Genre: Non-fiction
Word count: 1640

Overview

Buildings are all around us. This beautifully illustrated non-fiction text explores the history of building. In it, readers can find out about some amazing buildings, how they were made and why. It tells how walls were built to protect countries from enemies, and how the earliest building materials were developed. We discover how people learned to build taller, stronger buildings and even how to build houses on water.

The book is a companion text to 'Ships and Boats and Things that Float' (Purple Band) which children may have read earlier in *Cambridge Reading Adventures*. Non-fiction features include a detailed glossary as well as many labels and captions which add further information to that featured in the main body of the text. A simple map enables readers to locate the places where these amazing buildings can be found.

Learning outcomes

Children can:

- search for and find information in texts more flexibly
- sustain interest in longer, more complex texts
- express opinions, considering authorial intent and interpretation.

Developing reading comprehension

- Children can select areas of personal interest to research, learning how to pose questions and locate information in the text to provide the answer.
- Page layout is varied as appropriate for purpose (see for example, pages 22 and 23). Children will need to recognise and understand how page layout and design supports comprehension of text, or provides additional information.

Grammar and sentence structure

- Longer sentence structures containing two or more ideas and punctuated using commas.
- Adjectives and adverbial phrases are used to create effect or provide emphasis: '*fantastic shaped domes*'; '*the biggest wooden church in the world*'.

Word meaning and spelling

- Subject-specific vocabulary is supported by the glossary.
- Labels and captions provide additional information to support meaning.

Curriculum links

History – The book could be used in conjunction with studies of particular historical periods, alongside other non-fiction texts and websites.

Art – Children can experiment with different building materials to design and create their own house – what features would they really like to include?

WHITE BAND

Title: The Great Migration
Authors: Jonathan and Angela Scott

Genre: Non-fiction
Word count: 1077

Overview

Using stunning, real-life photography, this non-fiction text tells of the movement of animals throughout the year from the Serengeti plains to the Masai Mara Game Reserve. The Great Migration is a round trip of 3000 kilometres. Readers find out why wildebeests and other animals make this journey, and the dangers they face on the way.

The text is beginning to widen the range of genre and writing styles, and employs both recount and non-chronological report conventions. Information is more detailed and is conveyed using a range of non-fiction features (diagrams, maps, time-lines). Specialised vocabulary is defined in a glossary.

Learning outcomes

Children can:

- read silently most of the time
- search for and find information in texts more flexibly
- show increased awareness of vocabulary and precise meaning
- express reasoned opinions about what is read, and compare texts.

Developing reading comprehension

- Children can select areas of personal interest to research, learning how to pose questions and locate information in the text to provide the answer.
- Use summarizing skills to retell the events of the Great Migration in sequence. Refer to the time-line (on pages 28 and 29) to confirm this. What would children consider to be the most significant event of the Great Migration, and why?

Grammar and sentence structure

- Sentence structures are longer with more subordinate phrases or clauses (e.g.' *As more animals arrive, they become more and more uneasy and nervous.*').
- Time and causal connectives are used to navigate the reader through events (e.g. '*Soon they must be ready ...*'; '*the herds cannot stay here too long because there is not enough grass.*').
- Adverbial phrases (e.g. '*further north*', '*as soon as*') provide cohesion as events unfold.

Word meaning and spelling

- The text contains specific technical and topic language ('*waterhole*', '*migration*', '*minerals*').
- New vocabulary is supported by the glossary and the non-fiction text features, such as labels and captions.

Curriculum links

Geography – Use atlases, globes and websites to find Tanzania and Kenya and to track the migration across the seasons (see page 8).

Social studies – It is not only animals that migrate. People also migrate as they move to a new area or country. Why do we move? Do we always want to? There are also possible links to religious texts that consider the mass movement of people.

WHITE BAND

Title: The Mobile Continent
Author: Chris Oxlade

Genre: Non-fiction
Word count: 1160

Overview

People use their phones for all kinds of things; for sending emails, watching videos and even paying their bills. In this book, children find out about how phones are helping make Africa become the 'Mobile Continent'. The book traces the development of the mobile phone and its use in Africa.

This is a non-fiction text, predominantly written in the report genre, with elements of explanatory text (as on pages 8 and 10).

Learning outcomes

Children can:

- tackle novel, unfamiliar words, monitor their own understanding, searching for help in the text when necessary
- search for and find information in texts, using a range of non-fiction text features
- sustain interest across a longer text, employing comprehension strategies to enable them to return to it after a break.

Developing reading comprehension

- The title is a play on words and teachers will need to ensure this is understood by the children.
- A wide range of non-fiction text features support the meaning, or provide the information in an alternate form (such as the diagram on page 10).

Grammar and sentence structure

- Sentence structures are longer, and include subordinate phrases or clauses, for example: *'It can do lots more jobs than a simple mobile phone, but it is more expensive to buy'* (page 6).
- There is some variation in sentence length to create effect or add emphasis (for example, on page 4: *'It uses radio instead'*).
- Sentences are written as appropriate to a report text using a generic style and present tense verbs.

Word meaning and spelling

- Technical language is used. This is explained by the glossary, supported by captions and labels, and contextualised to establish meaning.

Curriculum links

History – This text will support work on the development of human communication methods around the world.

Science and Nature – Carry out experiments related to sound, such as using tin cans and string to convey messages from one child to another.

PSHE – The importance of keeping in touch and the purpose of communication is explored in this text. Children could explore reasons for communicating with others: for help, friendship, providing information, etc. and ways in which they communicate with family and friends.

Mapping and Correlation Chart

Mapping and Correlation Chart (Book Bands GREEN to WHITE)

Band	Title	Fiction/non-fiction	Author	Cambridge Primary objectives	International Primary Curriculum links	IB Primary Years Program topic links	Cambridge Global English Unit links
GREEN	Take Zayan with You!	F	Peter Millett	Identify and describe story settings and characters. Talk about what happens at the beginning, in the middle or at the end of a story.	Milepost 1 Who am I?; Forces	Who we are	Grade 1 Unit 3 Fun and games Grade 2 Unit 3 Ready, steady, go!
GREEN	Hide and Seek	F	Lynne Rickards	Anticipate what happens next in a story. Make simple inferences about characters and events to show understanding.	Milepost 1 I'm Alive	Who we are	Grade 1 Unit 3 Fun and games
GREEN	The Lion and the Mouse	F	Vivian French	Use phonic knowledge to read decodable words. Read aloud from simple books independently.	Milepost 1 The stories people tell	Who we are	Grade 2 Unit 2 Good neighbours
GREEN	Turtle is a Hero	F	Gabby Pritchard	Make simple inferences about characters and events to show understanding. Read aloud from simple books independently.	Milepost 1 A Day in the Life	Who we are	Grade 2 Unit 2 Good neighbours
GREEN	Baking Bread	NF	Lynne Rickards	Read labels, lists and captions to find information. Aware that texts for different purposes look different.	Milepost 1 We are what we eat	How the world works; How we organize ourselves	Grade 1 Unit 4 Making things
GREEN	Big Bugs	NF	Claire Llewellyn	Read labels, lists and captions to find information. Know the parts of a book, e.g. title page, contents.	Milepost 1 Flowers and insects	How the world works	Grade 2 Unit 6 Bugs: Fact and fiction
GREEN	A Drop of Rain	NF	Tanya Landman	Use phonic knowledge to read decodable words. Anticipate what happens next in a story.	Milepost 1 Science - Water world	How the world works	Grade 1 Unit 8 Wonderful water
GREEN	Dressing for the Weather	NF	Kathryn Harper	Read labels, lists and captions to find information. Aware that texts for different purposes look different.	Milepost 1 All dressed up	Where we are in place and time	Grade 1 Unit 8 Wonderful water Grade 2 Unit 4 The big sky
ORANGE	Omar in Trouble	F	Gabby Pritchard	Talk about what happens at the beginning, in the middle or at the end of a story. Predict story endings.	Milepost 1 Art	Who we are; How we express ourselves	Grade 1 Unit 4 Making things
ORANGE	For Today, For Tomorrow	F	Lauri Kubuitsile	Make simple inferences from the words on the page. Predict story endings.	Milepost 1 Things people do	How we organize ourselves'	n/a
ORANGE	Sang Kancil and Crocodile	F	Jim Carrington	Make simple inferences from the words on the page. Predict story endings.	Milepost 1 The stories people tell	Where we are in place and time	n/a
ORANGE	The Great Inventor	F	Gabby Pritchard	Read aloud with increased accuracy, fluency and expression. Talk about what happens at the beginning, in the middle or at the end of a story.	Milepost 1 History – People of the Past; A Day in the Life	How the world works	Grade 1 Unit 4 Making things

Band	Title	Fiction/non-fiction	Author	Cambridge Primary objectives	International Primary Curriculum links	IB Primary Years Program topic links	Cambridge Global English Unit links
ORANGE	The Best Little Bullfrog in the Forest	F	Ian Whybrow	Make simple inferences from the words on the page. Comment on some vocabulary choices, e.g. adjectives.	Milepost 1 Who am I?	How the world works	n/a
ORANGE	Life on the Reef	NF	Andy Belcher	Make simple inferences from the words on the page. Find answers to questions by reading a section of text.	Milepost 1 Water World; Science- Earth - our home	How the world works	Grade 1 Unit 8 Wonderful water
ORANGE	Super Malls	NF	Anita Ganeri	Locate words by initial letter in simple dictionaries, glossaries and indexes. Find factual information from different formats, e.g. charts, labelled diagrams.	Milepost 1 Buildings	How we organize ourselves	Grade 2 Unit 9 Inside and outside cities
ORANGE	Town Underground	NF	Jonathan Emmett	Locate words by initial letter in simple dictionaries, glossaries and indexes. Find answers to questions by reading a section of text.	Milepost 1 Buildings; Science - Earth - Our home; People of the Past	Where we are in place and time	Grade 2 Unit 8 Home, sweet home
TURQUOISE	The Power Cut	F	Peter Millett	Read aloud with increased accuracy, fluency and expression. Talk about what happens at the beginning, in the middle or at the end of a story.	Milepost 1 Science - It's Shocking!	How the world works	Grade 3 Unit 1 Working together
TURQUOISE	Sang Kancil and the Tiger	F	Jim Carrington	Read aloud with increased accuracy, fluency and expression. Identify and describe story settings and characters.	Milepost 1 The stories people tell; Habitats	Who we are	n/a
TURQUOISE	Sinbad Goes to Sea	F	Ian Whybrow	Read aloud with increased accuracy, fluency and expression. Identify and describe story settings and characters.	Milepost 1 The stories people tell; A Day in the Life; From A to B; Hooray…Let's Go on Holiday	Where we are in place and time	n/a
TURQUOISE	The Great Jewelled Egg Mystery	F	Gabby Pritchard	Read aloud with increased accuracy, fluency and expression. Comment on some vocabulary choices, e.g. adjectives.	Milepost 1 The stories people tell	Who we are	Grade 3 Unit 1 Working together
TURQUOISE	How Chocolate is Made	NF	Claire Llewellyn	Read and follow simple instructions, e.g. in a recipe. Find factual information from different formats, e.g. charts, labelled diagrams.	Milepost 2 Chocolate; Milepost 1 We are what we eat	How the world works	Grade 3 Unit 1 Working together
TURQUOISE	Draw the World	NF	Catherine Chambers	Read and follow simple instructions, e.g. in a recipe. Identify general features of known text types.	Milepost 1 Art	How we express ourselves	Grade 3 Unit 7 Puzzles and code
TURQUOISE	Motorcycles	NF	Andy Belcher	Find answers to questions by reading a section of text. Find factual information from different formats, e.g. charts.	Milepost 1 From A to B	Who we are; How the world works	Grade 3 Unit 5 Inventors and inventions

Band	Title	Fiction/non-fiction	Author	Cambridge Primary objectives	International Primary Curriculum links	IB Primary Years Program topic links	Cambridge Global English Unit links
TURQUOISE	Clever Computers	NF	Jonathan Emmett	Locate words by initial letter in simple dictionaries, glossaries and indexes. Find answers to questions by reading a section of text.	Milepost 1 Media Magic - Communication	Where we are in place and time; How the world works	Grade 3 Unit 5 Inventors and inventions Grade 3 Unit 7 Puzzles and codes
PURPLE	Sandstorm	F	Peter Millett	Identify and describe story settings and characters. Comment on some vocabulary choices, e.g. adjectives.	Milepost 1 From A to B	How the world works	Grade 3 Unit 3 The desert
PURPLE	Sinbad and the Roc	F	Ian Whybrow	Identify and describe story settings and characters. Comment on some vocabulary choices, e.g. adjectives.	Milepost 1 The Stories People tell ; From A to B	Where we are in place and time	n/a
PURPLE	King Fox	F	Tom Bradman	Begin to infer meanings beyond the literal, e.g. about motives and character. Identify the main points or gist of a text.	Milepost 1 The Stories People tell	Who we are	Grade 3 Unit 2 Good neighbours
PURPLE	Going on a Plane	NF	Alison Sage	Find answers to questions by reading a section of text. Find factual information from different formats, e.g. charts, labelled diagrams.	Milepost 1 From A to B	How the world works	Grade 2 Unit 9 Inside and outside cities
PURPLE	Ships, Boats and Things that Float	NF	Scoular Anderson	Locate words by initial letter in simple dictionaries, glossaries.	Milepost 1 What's it made of; From A to B	How the world works	Grade 3 Unit 5 Inventors and inventions
PURPLE	Pterosaur!	NF	Jon Hughes	Answer questions referring to single points in text. Locate information in non-fiction texts using contents page and index.	Milepost 2 Footprints from the past	Where we are in place and time	Grade 3 Unit 6 Dinosaurs
PURPLE	The Book of World Facts	NF	Anita Ganeri	Locate words by initial letter in simple dictionaries, glossaries and indexes. Find factual information from different formats, e.g. charts, labelled diagrams.	Milepost 1 Our world	Where we are in place and time	Grade 3 Unit 3 The desert Grade 3 Unit 4 Look again
GOLD	Tefo and the Lucky Football Boots	F	Lauri Kubuitsile	Note how text is organised into sections or chapters. Read aloud with expression to engage the listener.	Milepost 2 Shaping up	Who we are	Grade 4 Unit 1 Family circles
GOLD	Yu and the Great Flood	F	Tony Bradman	Read aloud with expression to engage the listener. Begin to infer meanings beyond the literal, e.g. about motives and character.	Milepost 1 The stories people tell; Milepost 2 Significant people	Sharing the planet	Grade 4 Unit 2 Stories
GOLD	Lost at Sea	F	Peter Millett	Note how text is organised into sections or chapters. Consider words that make an impact, e.g. adjectives.	Milepost 2 Explorers and adventurers	How the world works	Grade 4 Unit 5 Getting around
GOLD	Animals of the Ice Age	NF	Jon Hughes	Locate information in non-fiction texts using contents page and index. Consider ways that information is set out on page.	Milepost 2 Footprints from the past; History - Scavengers and Settlers	How the world works	n/a
GOLD	Scarface: The Real Lion King	NF	Jonathan and Angela Scott	Locate information in non-fiction texts using contents page and index. Identify the main purpose of a text.	Milepost 1 Science - The Nature of Life	How the world works	Grade 4 Unit 1 Family circles

Band	Title	Fiction/non-fiction	Author	Cambridge Primary objectives	International Primary Curriculum links	IB Primary Years Program topic links	Cambridge Global English Unit links
GOLD	Giants of the Ocean	NF	Catherine Bowley	Answer questions referring to single points in text. Locate information in non-fiction texts using contents page and index.	Milepost 2 Science –The Nature of Life	How the world works	Grade 3 Unit 9 Big and little
GOLD	Rags to Bags	NF	Anita Ganeri	Locate information in non-fiction texts using contents page and index. Consider ways that information is set out on page.	Milepost 2 Fashion; Young Entrepeneurs	Sharing the planet	Grade 3 Unit 5 Inventors and inventions
WHITE	The Great Escape	F	Peter Millett	Consider words that make an impact, e.g. adjectives. Answer questions referring to single points in text.	Milepost 2 Science - Land, sea and sky	Who we are	Grade 3 Unit 9 Big and little
WHITE	Mei and the Pirate Queen	F	Tony Bradman	Begin to infer meanings beyond the literal, e.g. about motives and character. Consider words that make an impact, e.g. adjectives.	Milepost 2 They made a difference	Sharing the planet	Grade 4 Unit 2 Stories
WHITE	The Silk Road	F	Tony Bradman	Note how text is organised into sections or chapters. Read aloud with expression to engage the listener.	Milepost 2 Young Entrepeneurs	Where we are in place and time	Grade 4 Unit 2 Stories
WHITE	Earthquakes	NF	Kathryn Harper	Consider ways that information is set out on page. Identify the main purpose of a text.	Milepost 2 Active Planet	How the world works	n/a
WHITE	Sticks and Bricks and Bits of Stone	NF	Scoular Anderson	Locate information in non-fiction texts using contents page. Consider ways that information is set out on page.	Milepost 2 Treasure; History - Temples Tombs and Treasures	Where we are in place and time	Grade 4 Unit 4 Homes
WHITE	The Mobile Continent	NF	Chris Oxlade	Locate information in non-fiction texts using contents page and index. Consider ways that information is set out on page.	Milepost 2 Inventions that changed the world	How the world works; How we organize ourselves	Grade 3 Unit 5 Inventors and inventions
WHITE	The Great Migration	NF	Jonathan and Angela Scott	Consider ways that information is set out on page. Locate information in non-fiction texts using contents page and index.	Milepost 2 Do you live around here?	Where we are in place and time	Grade 3 Unit 3 The desert

SECTION 3: READING ASSESSMENT

Reading Assessment

Successful guided reading relies on the texts being at just the right instructional level: the child needs to read the book with a degree of independence but with some challenges and opportunity for new learning to be taught in the guided reading lesson. If the book is too easy, no new learning can occur. If it is too difficult, then comprehension breaks down completely. *Cambridge Reading Adventures* includes a Benchmark text at each band. To ascertain that a child is ready to progress to the next band, teachers carry out the benchmark assessment, beginning with an individual running record of continuous text reading.

Taking a running record

Give the child a copy of the book. The text will have been unseen before this point. Follow the instructions on the record sheet, providing an overview of the book and locating the place to start the reading.

As the child reads, record the reading behaviour using the following procedures:

Tick each word read correctly	✓ ✓ ✓ ✓ ✓ 'The baby duck can walk,' ✓ ✓ ✓ said Grey Mouse.
Record incorrect responses above the word and record as an error.	✓ ✓ ✓ ✓ run 'The baby duck can walk,' ✓ ✓ ✓ said Grey Mouse.
Record any successful self-corrections by writing **SC** next to the original error. Record as a self-correction.	✓ ✓ ✓ ✓ run | SC 'The baby duck can walk,' ✓ ✓ ✓ said Grey Mouse.
Use a dash when a child omits a word or gives no response. This is counted as an error.	✓ - ✓ ✓ ✓ 'The baby duck can walk,' ✓ ✓ ✓ said Grey Mouse.
If a child inserts a word, write it into the running record. This is counted as an error.	✓ little ✓ ✓ ✓ 'The/baby duck can walk,' ✓ ✓ ✓ said Grey Mouse.
Record **T** if you decide to tell the child the correct word. This is counted as an error.	✓ ✓ ✓ ✓ run | 'The baby duck can walk,' | T ✓ ✓ - | said Grey Mouse. | T
Record **A** if the child appeals to you for help if unsure of a word or after an incorrect response. Encourage them to try. Record **SC** if the child is able to read the word, or tell them the word, recording **T** and counting this as an error	✓ ✓ ✓ ✓ - | A 'The baby duck can walk,' | T ✓ ✓ mum | A | SC said Grey Mouse.
Record **R** above the word if the child repeats it. Indicate the number of times the word is reread. Repetition is **not** counted as an error.	✓ ✓R ✓ ✓ ✓ 'The baby duck can walk,' ✓R² ✓ ✓ said Grey Mouse.

Record **R** with an arrow if the child reads back in the sentence and repeats more than one word. Rereading is **not** counted as an error.	✓ ✓ ✓R ✓ ✓ 'The baby duck can walk,' ✓ ✓ ✓ said Grey Mouse.
If the child becomes confused, stop the reading and say 'Try that again'. Bracket the confused passage and write **TTA**. This is counted as an error.	[✓ ✓ — is running] TTA 'The baby duck can walk,' ✓ ✓ ✓ said Grey Mouse.

Scoring a running record

The aim of this benchmarking assessment is to ascertain whether the child is ready to move to the next band. To do so, a child would need to be reading at around 94% accuracy at the current band.

Finding an accuracy rate

Look at your running record of the child's reading behaviours. Total how many errors you recorded in the errors column (see page 85 for a completed example).

Divide the total number of words by the number of errors in the running record to find the error ratio:

> **64** (words in the running record)
> divided by **6** (number of errors)
> = a ratio of **1:10**

Next, convert the ratio to an accuracy rate, using the table below:

Error ratio	Accuracy rate	
1:100	99%	
1:50	98%	Easy: At 95% and above, indicates that texts are easy for the child to read at this band.
1:35	97%	
1:25	96%	
1:20	95%	
1:17	94%	Instructional: At between 90% - 94%, texts are read more accurately, with fluency and understanding, whilst an element of challenge remains.
1:14	93%	
1:12.5	92%	
1:11.75	91%	
1:10	90%	
1:9	89%	Hard: Below 90%, the reading becomes too difficult: the child is unable to problem-solve effectively and comprehension breaks down
1:8	87.5%	
1:7	85.5%	
1:6	83%	
1:5	80%	

> An error ratio of 1: 10
> converts to an accuracy rate of 90%

Record the accuracy rate on the running record form, indicating if this text is at an easy, instructional or hard level for this child.

Finding the self-correction rate

Total the number of self-corrections recorded in the second column (page 85 provides an example). Remember, self-corrections are not errors; they indicate reading behaviours the child has initiated independently.

To calculate the self-correction rate, add together the total number of errors and the total number of self-corrections. Then, divide this figure by the number of self-corrections only:

> **9** (Total number of errors and self-corrections)
> divided by **3** (number of self-corrections)
> = a self-correction ratio of **1:3**

Record this information on the running record form.

Reading Assessment

Analysing the child's reading behaviours

An accuracy rate will give a comparable measure of progress, but it does not provide information about the reading behaviours the child is using and how effective these are. These reading behaviours, or strategies, are indicators of how the child is using what he knows to process text. By analysing the reading behaviours captured on the running record, teachers can look more closely at what sources of information the child is using or neglecting.

Clay[10] identified three sources of information readers attend to when reading:

> **The meaning** – the information gained from knowledge about the subject or story, or from the supportive illustrations - does what has been read make sense?
>
> A child reading:
>
> ✓ ✓ bird ✓ ✓
> 'The baby duck can walk'
>
> is likely to have been led by meaning.

> **The syntax** – the support offered by grammatical language structures and punctuation: does what has been read sound right?
>
> A child reading:
>
> ✓ ✓ ✓ is ✓
> 'The baby duck can walk'
>
> may well be using the grammatical sentence structure up to that point in the sentence.

> **The visual information** – the letters and words in print on the page - does what has been read look right?
>
> A child reading:
>
> ✓ ✓ dog ✓ ✓
> 'The baby duck can walk'
>
> has noticed the first letter 'd' so has used a source of print information at error.

---

[10] Clay, M. M. (2013). *An Observation Survey of Early Literacy Achievement*. 3rd Edition. Auckland, N.Z.: Heinemann

When these three sources of information are in balance, reading is accurate. Children's reading errors reveal if they are relying on one source predominantly, or if they are neglecting to use one source effectively. This will change over time.

Of course, sometimes children may use more than one cue source at a time. As teachers, we can never know exactly what caused a child to make an error. We can only observe the behaviour and consider the most effective way to help that child solve the problem.

Analysing self-correction

Self-corrections are not errors; however, in order to fully understand what led the child to self-correct, we first have to analyse the error that led to that self-correction. Again, this cannot be certain – we can only make an assumption based on what we know of the child's previous reading response and the challenges in this particular text.

A child reading:

✓ ✓ dog | SC ✓ ✓
The baby duck | can walk

is likely to have used the initial letter as a source of visual information but self-corrected based on the meaning of the text, knowing the story is about a duck, cross-referencing to the pictures of the duck to support that meaning.

A child reading:

✓ ✓ ✓ is | SC ✓
The baby duck can | walk

is probably using visual information to self-correct a syntactic error that sounded right at the point of error but didn't look right.

Completing the running record analysis

First, look at all the errors, including those that were then self-corrected. Consider what sources of information the child was using at the point the error occurred.

Decide if the error was lead predominantly by meaning **(M)**, or by the sentence structure and grammar **(S)** or by the visual information **(V)**, or a combination of any of these. For example, an error can often call upon meaning and syntax, such as the child reading 'run' for 'walk'. Record the errors at each source of information in the first set of grey columns **'Error Analysis'**. Please note that omissions and insertions, whilst still counting as errors, are not analysed.

Now look back at initial errors that were then self-corrected. Follow the same procedure, recording as M, S and/or V to consider what sources of information the child used that led to formulating a correct response. Record each source of information used to self-correct in the second set of grey columns **'S/C Analysis'**.

There is a worked example of a running record analysis on page 85.

Comprehension assessment

Cambridge Reading Adventures benchmark assessments also provide teachers with opportunity to consider progression in comprehension. Comprehension skills are developmental and the complexity aligns with that of a child's literacy development.

Benchmark texts are designed to support teachers assess that development. Question prompts are provided to help assess understanding.

The comprehension assessment takes place **after** the text has been read and the running record taken. Begin by asking the child to retell the story in his own words. This will have been an unseen text. Retelling will help the teacher assess how well the child is able to demonstrate understanding.

Questions to assess understanding

Recalling: At the Early stage, comprehension questions are predominantly **recalling questions**, like those designed to assess *'What can Baby Duck do?'*; the answers are literal and can be specifically drawn from the text. Answers need to be accurate although sometimes there will be multiple choices.

Inferring: As children progress through the bands, the balance shifts to a greater proportion of **inferring questions**, such as *'Why do you think Brown Mouse and Grey Mouse shouted 'Help!'* which require children to read 'between the lines' of the specific information in the text in order to draw conclusions and to gain meaning. There will often be more than one plausible response.

Responding: Children develop their comprehension skills further in the Transitional stage. There will be fewer recalling questions. Now children are asked to 'go beyond the text' to explain, evaluate and comment on the content, and to demonstrate links with other texts they have read. There will often be multiple, plausible and reasonable responses to these **responding questions** such as *'Did you like this story? Can you tell me why/why not?'* Teachers will make a judgement based on the quality of the explanation and their knowledge of the child.

The chart below demonstrates how the balance of types of question develops from Early to Transitional bands.

Band	Recalling	Inferring	Responding
Pink A	3	1	
Pink B	3	1	
Red	3	1	
Yellow	3	2	1
Blue	3	2	1
Green	3	2	1
Orange	3	3	1
Turquoise	3	3	1
Purple	2	3	2
Gold	2	3	2
White	2	3	2

Progression of questions in *Cambridge Reading Adventures* Benchmark Texts

Score the number of questions answered correctly on the assessment summary.

Reading Assessment

Completing the Benchmark Assessment Summary

The Benchmark Assessment Summary is designed to pull together all the information gathered from the running record analysis, comprehension questions and from the teacher's own observations during the assessment. Based on this information, teachers will decide whether a child is ready to progress to the next band, or make recommendations to target particular aspects of language or reading behaviours whilst remaining at the current band. Page 86 provides a worked example.

Summary of observations during the assessment

Reading Strategies:

Record the error and self-correction rates on the summary form.

Looking at your analysis of errors and self corrections, consider:

- Did you notice a particular pattern of responses? For example, did the child overlook letter and word information in their errors?
- Are there any successful self-corrections? What were the sources of information that resulted in successful self-correction? Did the child look more carefully at the print information, perhaps? Or did they realise that it didn't make sense?
- Did the child try to make their reading make sense? Did they attempt to sound out or use parts of words to work things out?
- If the child is ready to begin working at the next band, you will see evidence of the child trying to work things out and in the majority of cases, making errors that make sense.

Using Print:

Particularly at the Early stage, print concepts are being established. It is important to note:

- How well did the child control left-to-right directionality and the return sweep on texts with multiple lines?
- Was one-to-one matching secure?
- Did the child read along the words, slowly checking and sounding out words which are phonically regular?
- Did the child notice and use chunks in words of more than one syllable?
- Were print features (such as commas, speech punctuation, layout) noticed and used?

A child that is regularly making errors with using print is not yet ready to read more challenging material and needs further work at the current band.

Fluency:

There is a clear link between fluency and comprehension. Children who read slowly and in a disjointed way often don't understand what they are reading. Things to note on your record are:

- Was the child reading in a phrased, fluent manner or was the reading disjointed and staccato-sounding?
- Was finger-pointing slowing the reading down?
- Did the child attend to punctuation to support reading for meaning?
- Was intonation appropriate?
- Were clues in print (such as words in bold or italic for emphasis) used for expression?

Summary of Reading Comprehension skills:

Retelling task:

- Could the child retell the text independently? Did the child embellish and add further information?
- To what extent did he rely on the pictures in the text to support the retelling? Were the pictures interpreted correctly?
- Did you have to prompt or assist in order to complete the retelling?
- Was the retelling confident and succinct?

Sequencing ideas:

- How well was the retelling structured?
- Were events followed in sequence?
- Were all the main events included?
- Was notice taken of additional events, subsidiary to the main events?

Control of vocabulary

- Was the vocabulary appropriate?
- Did it relate to the book?
- Did the child seek to explain or expand upon subject-specific vocabulary?
- Did it match the tone, style or genre of the text read?

Comprehension

Add the comprehension outcomes for recalling, inferring and responding, as appropriate.

Note down any particular information about how the child approached the comprehension questions, for example:

- Did he carefully reference back to the text to support his answers?
- Does he have difficulty in moving beyond the more literal questions?
- Was he misled by illustrations when information needed to answer the question was not pictured explicitly?

Think about what might have led the child to an incorrect response, and consider the plausibility of the answer.

Recommendations

This section enables the teacher to review the observations and consider the next steps for this child. The teacher will then need to look at the text characteristics for the next band, (see page 18 in this Teaching and Assessment Guide), and decide, on the basis of the evidence collected, whether the child is ready to progress.

NB: This judgement is not made on the accuracy rate alone, but by looking across all the elements of reading and comprehension assessed at each benchmark point.

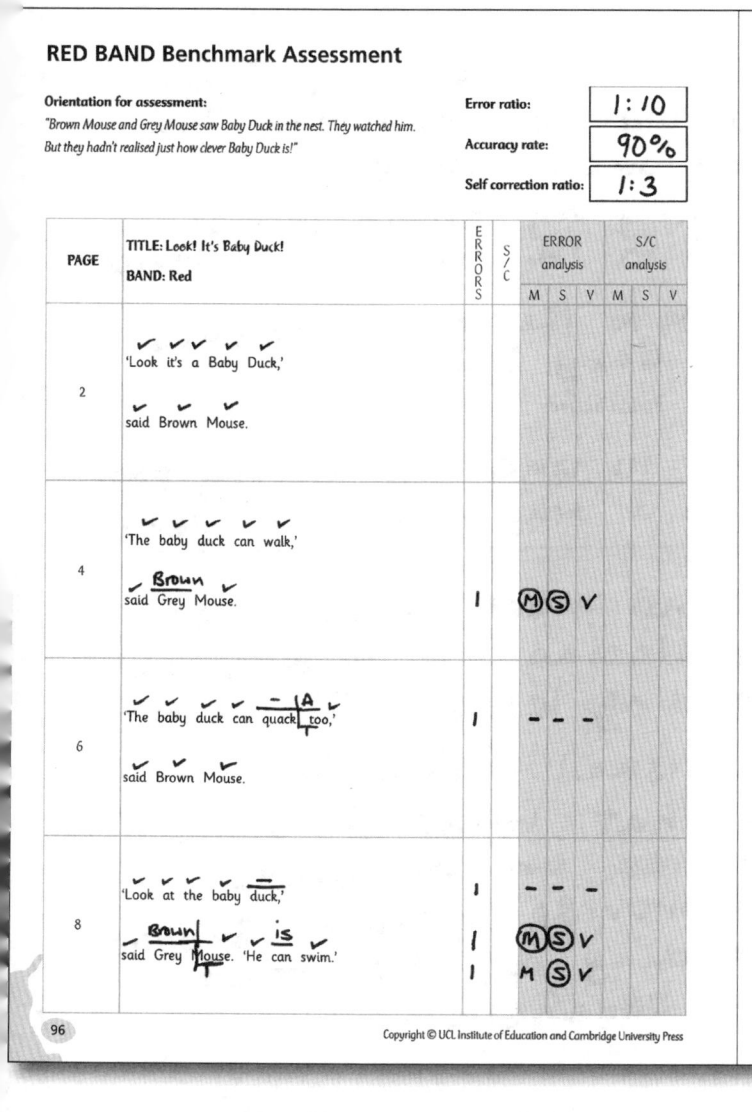

Reading Assessment

RED BAND Benchmark Assessment
Benchmark Assessment Summary
Look! It's Baby Duck

NAME: Aisha
CLASS GROUP: Tigers
DATE: 5th Feb. 2015

Accuracy:

- [ ] HARD — Errors: more than 1:10
- [x] INSTRUCTIONAL — Errors: between 1:10 and 1:25
- [ ] EASY — Errors: fewer than 1:25

Summary of Observations during the assessment

Reading Strategies: Errors predominantly meaning-led with SC using print information. Syntax mostly maintained. Grammatical errors indicate she is using sentence structure to predict.

Using Print: Aisha mostly controls 1-1 matching, with some mismatches when meaning overrides print information. Finger pointing used occasionally.

Fluency: The story sounded good and was phrased appropriately.

Summary of Reading Comprehension Skills

Retelling task: Some confusion about what each of the mice said. Ending was omitted and the focus was mainly on Baby Duck's actions.

Sequencing ideas: Difficulty in identifying Brown Mouse and Grey Mouse + their roles in the story. The build-up of events was not clear.

Control of vocabulary: Vocab used was appropriate to the text. Sometimes used 'Baby' rather than 'Baby Duck'.

Comprehension:

Recalling: ①/3   Inferring: ⓪/1   Total Score: ①

Comments: Aisha did not seem to understand why the Baby Duck shouted, or why the mice were scared.

Recommendations:

Aisha now needs to attend more closely to print to support her developing use of meaning + structure. In guided reading lessons, I will need to draw her attention to visual mismatches, prompting her to check that what she says matches what she can see on the page. Texts at Red band will provide greater support, and further guided reading at this band will be beneficial.

Move to Yellow Band? Y / **N**

Book Bands Class Progress Tracker / Transitional Reading

Child's name	Green	Orange	Turquoise	Purple	Gold	White
Child's name	Green	Orange	Turquoise	Purple	Gold	White
Child's name	Green	Orange	Turquoise	Purple	Gold	White

GREEN BAND Benchmark Assessment

Error ratio:

Accuracy rate:

Orientation for assessment:
'In this story, Turtle and a little boy meet on the beach. At first, the little boy isn't sure if he likes Turtle. But he soon finds out that Turtle is a hero.'

Self correction ratio:

PAGE	TITLE: Turtle is a Hero BAND: Green	ERRORS	S/C	ERROR analysis			S/C analysis		
				M	S	V	M	S	V
	The child reads aloud until page 6. The teacher tells unknown words without explanation. Begin taking the running record at this point.								
6	Suddenly, Turtle felt a tap on his head. He opened one eye. 'Hello, little boy,' he said.								
7	'Wow!' gasped the boy. 'You can speak?' 'Of course,' said Turtle. 'Are you afraid?'								
8	'No, but you are huge!' said the boy. 'Your neck is long and you have flippers. Your skin is wrinkly, too. You must be a …'								
9	DINOSAUR!'								

Copyright © UCL Institute of Education and Cambridge University Press

		ERRORS	S/C	ERROR analysis			S/C analysis		
				M	S	V	M	S	V
10	Turtle laughed. 'I'm not a dinosaur,' he said. 'My flippers help me swim fast … this shell makes me strong … … and your skin would be wrinkly too if you lived in the sea.'								
11	The boy laughed. 'Yes,' he said. 'I would look just like an old man.' The boy touched Turtle's shell. 'I think your shell could be very useful,' he said.								
12	'Come and swim with us,' Shouted the boy's friends. The boy waved Goodbye and went to play with his friends. Turtle smiled and began to swim home.								

		ERRORS	S/C	ERROR analysis			S/C analysis		
				M	S	V	M	S	V
13	Suddenly, he heard the boy shout. 'HELP!' he cried. 'HELP ME!' The boy was in the sea! A big wave was coming. 'Hold on,' shouted Turtle.								
14	Turtle swam fast. His flippers helped him race through the sea. He dived deep … and then … … up he POPPED. The boy was sitting on Turtle's strong shell.								
15	'You saved me!' cried the boy. 'Turtle is a hero!' Turtle smiled. 'I am not a hero,' he said. 'But I am your friend.' The boy hugged Turtle. 'I'm so happy that you are my friend,' he said.								
No of words **299**	**TOTALS** Total the sources of information used in self corrections and errors.								

GREEN BAND Benchmark Assessment
Comprehension assessment
Turtle is a Hero

NAME:

CLASS GROUP:

DATE:

Retelling task: *(Tick and comment as appropriate)*

Retold independently. ☐

Retold using the pictures to support ☐

Retold with some adult support ☐

Sequencing Ideas: *(Tick and comment as appropriate)*

Followed the correct sequence of events ☐

Mentioned some of the events in sequence ☐

Events retold out of sequence ☐

Control of Vocabulary: *(Tick and comment as appropriate)*

Used vocabulary of the book and their own vocabulary appropriately and interchangeably ☐

Used the vocabulary of the book appropriately ☐

Unfocused or inaccurate use of vocabulary denoting lack of understanding ☐

Questioning to assess understanding *(Tick as appropriate)*

Recalling:

Where did Turtle swim? ☐

(in the deep green sea)

What did Turtle do when he got to the beach? ☐

(made a hole; went to sleep in the hot sand; found a cool place; yawned and closed his eyes)

What did Turtle do to save the little boy? ☐

(swam fast; dived deep; popped up in the water; let him sit on his strong shell)

Score: ☐

Inferring:

Why did the little boy think that Turtle was a dinosaur? ☐

(had body parts that look like a dinosaur - long neck, flippers, wrinkly skin, hard shell)

What did the little boy think about Turtle at the end of the story? ☐

(Turtle is a good friend; Turtle will keep him safe in the sea; Turtle will always save him; The little boy now likes Turtle even though he looks odd)

Score: ☐

Responding:

Turtle says at the end that he is not a hero. What do you think? Score: ☐

Total Score: ☐

Copyright © UCL Institute of Education and Cambridge University Press

GREEN BAND Benchmark Assessment

Benchmark Assessment Summary
Turtle is a Hero

NAME:

CLASS GROUP:

DATE:

Accuracy:

☐ **HARD**
Errors: more than 1:10

☐ **INSTRUCTIONAL**
Errors: between 1:10 and 1:25

☐ **EASY**
Errors; fewer than 1:25

Summary of Observations during the assessment

Reading Strategies:

Using Print:

Fluency:

Summary of Reading Comprehension Skills

Retelling task:

Sequencing ideas:

Control of vocabulary:

Comprehension:
Recalling: ☐ / 3   Inferring: ☐ / 2   Responding: ☐ / 1   Total Score: ☐ / 6

Comments:

Recommendations:

Move to Orange Band? Y/N

ORANGE BAND Benchmark Assessment

Error ratio:

Accuracy rate:

Orientation for assessment:
'Little Bullfrog and his mother are watching a talent contest in the forest.
Little Bullfrog wants to be in it. He wants to be best at something. What will he do?'

Self correction ratio:

PAGE	TITLE: The Best Little Bullfrog in the Forest BAND: Orange	ERRORS	S/C	ERROR analysis			S/C analysis		
				M	S	V	M	S	V
2	In the damp leaves on the floor of the forest, a little brown bullfrog sat with his mother. They were watching a talent contest. 'Can I be in it?' he asked.								
3	'You're too little and too ugly!' called Crested Cockatoo from up in a tree. 'You have lumpy brown skin! Not like my beautiful feathers. I am going to win the talent contest!'								
4	'Don't listen,' said his mother. 'He's showing off. You have lovely skin. Come on, let's go and find somewhere cool.' As they hopped through the forest, a green parrot with a big red beak flew past and sat on a branch. 'Look at that!' said the little bullfrog. 'I wish I could fly!'								

Copyright © UCL Institute of Education and Cambridge University Press

		ERRORS	S/C	ERROR analysis			S/C analysis		
				M	S	V	M	S	V
5	'I am the best at flying,' cried Great-Billed Parrot. 'My green and blue feathers are beautiful and my big bill is strong. I am going to win the talent contest!'								
6	'I wish I was best at something,' said the little bullfrog with a sigh. 'Don't be upset,' croaked his mother. 'Let's find somewhere cool.' They had not gone far when they found some doves singing. 'Can I join in?' asked the little bullfrog. 'I can sing.' The little bullfrog croaked a song.								
8	'What a horrible noise!' cooed a Zebra Dove up in the branches. 'Listen to **me**. Now, that is a sweet song.' 'Listen to **my** song,' called Spotted Dove. 'It is much sweeter! I am going to win the talent contest!' And off they flew.								

Copyright © UCL Institute of Education and Cambridge University Press

		ERRORS	S/C	ERROR analysis			S/C analysis		
				M	S	V	M	S	V
9	The little bullfrog was very upset. 'It's true,' he said. 'My song sounds like a burp.' 'You have a lovely voice,' said his mother. 'Come along. Let's go and catch some flies at the pool.' They had a swim and ate some bugs.								
	Stop taking the running record at this point. Ask the child to read on quietly to themselves until the end of the story before beginning the comprehension assessment tasks.								
No of words **285**	**TOTALS** Total the sources of information used in self corrections and errors.								

ORANGE BAND Benchmark Assessment

Comprehension assessment
The Best Little Bullfrog in the Forest

NAME:

CLASS GROUP:

DATE:

Retelling task: *(Tick and comment as appropriate)*	☐
Retold independently.	☐
Retold using the pictures to support	☐
Retold with some adult support	

Sequencing Ideas: *(Tick and comment as appropriate)*	☐
Followed the correct sequence of events	☐
Mentioned some of the events in sequence	☐
Events retold out of sequence	

Control of Vocabulary: *(Tick and comment as appropriate)*	☐
Used vocabulary of the book and their own vocabulary appropriately and interchangeably	☐
Used the vocabulary of the book appropriately	☐
Unfocused or inaccurate use of vocabulary denoting lack of understanding	

Questioning to assess understanding *(Tick as appropriate)*

Recalling: 3

Why did Parrot think he would win the talent contest? ☐
(He was the best at flying; He had beautiful feathers; He had a strong beak.)
How did White-lipped Pit-viper miss Little Bullfrog and his mother? ☐
(They dived into the water to escape him; They were too quick for him.)
Why was Komodo Dragon the most disgusting animal in the forest? ☐
(His smell was worse than Civet Cat's; He gobbled up Civet Cat.)

Score: ☐

Inferring: 3

How do we know that Little Bullfrog was not good at singing? ☐
(His voice sounds like a burp; He 'croaked' a song; The Zebra Dove said his singing was a horrible noise.)
Why did Little Bullfrog's mother say: 'Let's go and find somewhere cool.' ☐
*(Frogs need to keep their skin cool and damp; It was too warm for them in the forest.
Do not accept: They wanted to hide from the snake.)*
Look at the last line on page 17. It says Little Bullfrog felt very special. Why did he feel special, do you think? ☐
(His mother loved him; He was best at some things; He wasn't as bad as he thought.)

Score: ☐

Responding: 1

Turn to page 8. What do you notice about the writing on this page?
Why do you think the author has written the text like this? ☐
(He has used bold print to help us to read with expression; It shows us how the Zebra Dove would talk; The Zebra Dove thinks she is the best singer.)

Score: ☐

Total Score: ☐

ORANGE BAND Benchmark Assessment

NAME:

Benchmark Assessment Summary

CLASS GROUP:

The Best Little Bullfrog in the Forest

DATE:

Accuracy:

◯ **HARD**
Errors: more than 1:10

◯ **INSTRUCTIONAL**
Errors: between 1:10 and 1:25

◯ **EASY**
Errors; fewer than 1:25

Summary of Observations during the assessment

Reading Strategies:

Using Print:

Fluency:

Summary of Reading Comprehension Skills

Retelling the story:

Comprehension:
Recalling: ◯ / 3   Inferring: ◯ / 3   Responding: ◯ / 1   Total Score: ◯ / 6

Comments:

Recommendations:

Move to Turquoise Band? Y/N

TURQUOISE BAND Benchmark Assessment

Error ratio:

Orientation for assessment:
'Ashia and her brothers enjoyed listening to the mystery story in the bookshop. Now they have a mystery of their own to solve.'

Accuracy rate:

Self correction ratio:

PAGE	TITLE: The Great Jewelled Egg Mystery BAND: Turquoise	ERRORS	S/C	ERROR analysis			S/C analysis		
				M	S	V	M	S	V
	Ask the child to read pages 2 – 4 independently before you begin to take the Running Record. Discuss the story so far:								
6	'Do you remember the old man?' Aisha said. 'Nadim nearly knocked him over. He sat here. He must have left the bag.' 'Yes! I remember,' said Farid. 'He had a silver stick.' Nadim grinned. 'Let's search for this mystery man!'								
7	They looked in the shops near the fountain … … the shoe shop … … phone shop … … and café … … but they couldn't find the old man.								

		ERRORS	S/C	ERROR analysis			S/C analysis		
				M	S	V	M	S	V
8	'Look! Here's a map.' called Farid. 'Let's think about where he got the egg.' 'We haven't looked in the Craft Village yet,' said Aisha. 'Brilliant!' said Farid. 'The egg could be from there.'								
10	The children went to the Craft Village. They showed the egg to some of the shopkeepers. Nobody knew where it was from. Then Aisha saw a sign. 'Look,' she said. 'Look at the name of that shop!' 'The Treasure Palace,' read Nadim. 'That's the name on the bag,' gasped Farid.								
11	'This egg belongs to an old man,' said the shopkeeper. 'He has a silver stick.' 'That's him,' cried Farid. 'He's just left,' said the man. 'Hurry - you might catch him.'								

		ERRORS	S/C	ERROR analysis			S/C analysis		
				M	S	V	M	S	V
12	The children raced out of the shop, but the old man had disappeared. 'We have to go,' said Farid, sadly. 'Dad's waiting.'								
13	Aisha took the egg out of the bag. She pressed a ruby in the middle. The egg popped open. A beautiful bird sang a sad song. Everyone stopped to listen to the song								
	Stop taking the running record at this point. Ask the child to read on independently until the end of the story before beginning the comprehension assessment tasks.								
No of words **239**	**TOTALS** Total the sources of information used in self corrections and errors.								

TURQUOISE BAND Benchmark Assessment

NAME:

Comprehension assessment

CLASS GROUP:

The Great Jewelled Egg Mystery

DATE:

Retelling task: *(Tick and comment as appropriate)*	
Retold independently.	☐
Retold using the pictures to support	☐
Retold with some adult support	☐

Sequencing Ideas: *(Tick and comment as appropriate)*	
Followed the correct sequence of events	☐
Mentioned some of the events in sequence	☐
Events retold out of sequence	☐

Control of Vocabulary: *(Tick and comment as appropriate)*	
Used vocabulary of the book and their own vocabulary appropriately and interchangeably	☐
Used the vocabulary of the book appropriately	☐
Unfocused or inaccurate use of vocabulary denoting lack of understanding	☐

Questioning to assess understanding   *(Tick as appropriate)*

Recalling:

How would the children recognize the old man they were looking for? ☐
(He was carrying a silver stick.)

Who, or what, was Jenna? ☐
(The mechanical bird inside the jewelled egg belonging to the old man.)

Why had the old man taken the egg to the Treasure Palace in the first instance? ☐
(The mechanical bird was broken/lost its voice/couldn't sing; For the bird to be mended/fixed.)

Score: ☐

Inferring:

Look at page 3. How do you know that time has passed and the children have now heard the mystery story? ☐
(The children have left the bookshop; Nadim says that it was a good story.)

Why does Aisha open the jellewed egg (on page 13)? ☐
(So that the bird would begin to sing and the old man might hear it.)

Can you explain how the children thought to ask the man in the 'Treasure Palace'? ☐
(The bag containing the jewelled egg had the same name on it so it might have come from this shop.
Do not accept: The name on the bag was the same as the shop's name).

Score: ☐

Responding:

Describe why you think the author called this book 'The Great Jewelled Egg Mystery'.
((The children had to follow clues to trace the owner of the egg; They didn't know who the egg belonged to.
Do not accept: Aisha wanted to be a detective; The children listened to a mystery story.) Score: ☐

Total Score: ☐

Copyright © UCL Institute of Education and Cambridge University Press

TURQUOISE BAND Benchmark Assessment

NAME:

Benchmark Assessment Summary

CLASS GROUP:

The Great Jewelled Egg Mystery

DATE:

Accuracy:

☐ **HARD**
Errors: more than 1:10

☐ **INSTRUCTIONAL**
Errors: between 1:10 and 1:25

☐ **EASY**
Errors: fewer than 1:25

Summary of Observations during the assessment

Reading Strategies:

Using Print:

Fluency:

Summary of Reading Comprehension Skills

Retelling task:

Sequencing ideas:

Control of vocabulary:

Comprehension:
Recalling: ☐ / 3   Inferring: ☐ / 2   Responding: ☐ / 3   Total Score: ☐ / 6

Comments:

Recommendations:

Move to Purple Band? Y/N

PURPLE BAND Benchmark Assessment

Error ratio:

Accuracy rate:

Self correction ratio:

Orientation for assessment:
'One morning, Fox woke up late and felt hungry. He went out to see what he could eat for his breakfast. But the animals were too scared to share their food. They were hiding from Tiger. Will Fox ever get his breakfast?'

PAGE	TITLE: **King Fox** BAND: Purple	ERRORS	S/C	ERROR analysis			S/C analysis		
				M	S	V	M	S	V
2	Fox woke up late. He was hungry. He stretched and yawned and thought about the delicious fruit and nuts he could have for breakfast.								
3	'What a lovely day,' he said to himself.								
4	Still sleepy, Fox went to find something to eat. After looking for a while, he saw the squirrels hiding in some high branches. 'Hello,' he called up to them, with his sweetest grin. 'Have you got any nuts for my breakfast?'								
5	'Ssshhh! We're hiding,' one whispered back. 'Someone saw Tiger! You have to be quiet!' But Fox felt too hungry to be quiet and wait, so he carried on to find someone else.								

		ERRORS	S/C	ERROR analysis			S/C analysis		
				M	S	V	M	S	V
6	Fox went to the mice next, then the deer, and even the snakes, but no one wanted to help him find his breakfast. His stomach rumbled loudly. 'I'm so hungry,' he said, rubbing his stomach. 'I must find something to eat soon. Can today get any worse?'								
7	A huge growl answered his question. Tiger was standing just behind him. 'Oh-oh …'								
8	Before he could think 'huge, terrifying cat', Fox was running away. What a terrible day! All Fox wanted was his breakfast, and now he was going to be someone else's breakfast.								
9	Tiger was very fast. Fox looked behind him and all he could see was teeth. He dashed onto a forest track, right in front of a cart.								

Copyright © UCL Institute of Education and Cambridge University Press

		ERRORS	S/C	ERROR analysis			S/C analysis		
				M	S	V	M	S	V
10	Just in time, Fox leapt out of the way, into a bush. Shivering with fear, he looked around. Tiger had vanished, but Fox was too scared to move.								
11	The cart stopped, too. The driver had seen some foresters sitting on the track. He jumped out of the cart and started shouting.								
	Stop taking the running record at this point. Ask the child to read on quietly to themselves until the end of the story before beginning the comprehension assessment tasks.								
No of words **275**	**TOTALS** Total the sources of information used in self corrections and errors.								

PURPLE BAND Benchmark Assessment
Comprehension assessment
King Fox

NAME:

CLASS GROUP:

DATE:

Retelling task: *(Tick and comment as appropriate)*	
Retold independently.	☐
Retold using the pictures to support	☐
Retold with some adult support	☐

Sequencing Ideas: *(Tick and comment as appropriate)*	
Followed the correct sequence of events	☐
Mentioned some of the events in sequence	☐
Events retold out of sequence	☐

Control of Vocabulary: *(Tick and comment as appropriate)*	
Used vocabulary of the book and their own vocabulary appropriately and interchangeably	☐
Used the vocabulary of the book appropriately	☐
Unfocused or inaccurate use of vocabulary denoting lack of understanding	☐

Questioning to assess understanding *(Tick as appropriate)*

Recalling: 2
What might Fox want to eat for his breakfast? ☐
(fruit and nuts (from text); apples; strawberries (from illustrations))
What does Fox think when Tiger appears behind him (page 7)? ☐
(He thinks he is going to be eaten/be Tiger's breakfast; That he has to run away.)
Score: ☐

Inferring: 3
Why do the squirrels tell Fox he has to be quiet? ☐
(If he makes a noise, Tiger will hear him; If they keep quiet, Tiger won't know they are there.)
Why do you think the foresters were frightened of the man in yellow who sat at the back of the cart? ☐
(He was very important/the king/the owner of the cart; He was more important than the angry man.)
The animals give 'King Fox' lots of food, but are they really frightened of Fox? ☐
(No, but they want Tiger to go away; Fox says that he and Tiger will leave as soon as they have eaten, so they give him food; Fox is pretending to be strong, but the animals are more frightened of Tiger so they give him food to make him go away.)
Score: ☐

Responding: 2
Look at pages 14 and 15. How does the author's choice of words tell us about how Fox is feeling? ☐
(He is feeling scared, but trying to be brave; He knows he has to face Tiger; He thinks his idea will work)
Does this story remind you of any others you have read or heard? ☐
(Answers could include: Stories where foxes are cunning and trick other animals; Other animal stories with a similar setting; Other animals that are clever (such as Sang Kancil in Cambridge Reading Adventures); Similar artwork or design. Accept any reasonable comparison.)
Score: ☐

Total Score: ☐

PURPLE BAND Benchmark Assessment
Benchmark Assessment Summary
King Fox

NAME:

CLASS GROUP:

DATE:

Accuracy:

☐ **HARD**
Errors: more than 1:10

☐ **INSTRUCTIONAL**
Errors: between 1:10 and 1:25

☐ **EASY**
Errors; fewer than 1:25

Summary of Observations during the assessment

Reading Strategies:

Using Print:

Fluency:

Summary of Reading Comprehension Skills

Retelling the story:

Comprehension:
Recalling: ☐ / 2   Inferring: ☐ / 3   Responding: ☐ / 2   Total Score: ☐ / 7

Comments:

Recommendations:

Move to Gold Band? Y/N

Copyright © UCL Institute of Education and Cambridge University Press

GOLD BAND Benchmark Assessment

Error ratio:

Accuracy rate:

Orientation for assessment:
'Adeline and her father are in the middle of a storm out at sea. Adeline's father gets more and more worried. Will they be rescued?'

Self correction ratio:

PAGE	TITLE: LOST AT SEA BAND: Gold	ERRORS	S/C	ERROR analysis			S/C analysis		
				M	S	V	M	S	V
2	Adeline and her father bounced around In the heavy waves on their life raft. The same waves that had smashed Their boat now crashed down on top of them. They were lost at sea. Their sailing boat Had sunk after being hit by the huge storm. Mr Lee had a broken arm. Adeline had A cut on her head. 'Dad, are you okay?' Adeline cried. 'Yes, I'm alright,' Mr Lee said. 'Will we be okay in this life raft?' Adeline asked. 'I hope so,' Mr Lee replied.								
4	'Have we got any food?' Mr Lee asked. Adeline looked around. She found her lunch box. It had a slice of pizza inside it. 'This is all we have to eat,' she sighed. 'And we have no radio and no maps. Everything was lost overboard.'								

		ERRORS	S/C	ERROR analysis			S/C analysis		
				M	S	V	M	S	V
5	Mr Lee looked very worried. 'We are going to have to make that food last a really long time. Let's wait until we are starving before we eat it,' he said.								
6	Just then the life raft was knocked sideways. A huge black fin shot up out of the water. 'Oh no! It's a shark!' Mr Lee cried.								
7	Two more black fins shot up. Adeline covered her eyes.								
8	'Wait! They're not sharks,' Mr Lee cried. Adeline uncovered her eyes. 'Dad, you're right. Sharks aren't black - they're grey.' 'They're orcas,' Mr Lee cried. 'Thank goodness for that', Adeline gasped. The fins dipped back into the water and the whales swam off.								

Copyright © UCL Institute of Education and Cambridge University Press

		ERRORS	S/C	ERROR analysis			S/C analysis		
				M	S	V	M	S	V
10	Dad looked at his watch. 'Oh no, this is bad. Really bad. It's nearly midnight and no one knows we're out here alone!' 'Will someone find us?' said Adeline. 'They'd better...' Dad groaned. 'I'd hate to think what will happen if they don't.'								
	Stop taking the running record at this point. Ask the child to read on until the end of the story before beginning the comprehension assessment tasks.								
No of words **284**	**TOTALS** Total the sources of information used in self corrections and errors.								

GOLD BAND Benchmark Assessment
Comprehension assessment
LOST AT SEA

NAME:

CLASS GROUP:

DATE:

Retelling task: *(Tick and comment as appropriate)*

Retold independently. ☐

Retold using the pictures to support ☐

Retold with some adult support ☐

Sequencing Ideas: *(Tick and comment as appropriate)*

Followed the correct sequence of events ☐

Mentioned some of the events in sequence ☐

Events retold out of sequence ☐

Control of Vocabulary: *(Tick and comment as appropriate)*

Used vocabulary of the book and their own vocabulary appropriately and interchangeably ☐

Used the vocabulary of the book appropriately ☐

Unfocused or inaccurate use of vocabulary denoting lack of understanding ☐

Questioning to assess understanding *(Tick as appropriate)*

Recalling:

What had happened to their boat? ☐
(It had been sunk in the storm; The waves had crashed down on top of it.)

How did they get the ship to notice them? ☐
(Adeline made the piece of foil from the pizza flash like a mirror; They used the foil; They made the sun bounce off the foil; They used the foil to reflect the sunlight.)

Score: ☐

Inferring:

Why does Mr Lee tell Adeline not to eat the pizza at the beginning of the story? ☐
(They may not be rescued for a long time; They may have no more food for a long time; They should make their food last.)

Why does Adeline cover her eyes? ☐
(She thinks that there are sharks in the water; She doesn't want to see the sharks; She is frightened.)

How does Mr Lee know that they are going to be rescued? ☐
(The ship sounds its horn to signal; They have seen the flashing light.)

Score: ☐

Responding:

Look at page 17. It says 'Suddenly her face lit up?' What do you think the author means? ☐
(That Adeline has an idea; That she knows what to do. NOT That a light shone on her face.)

Do you think Adeline and her father were brave? Why/Why not? ☐
*(Yes: They didn't panic; They stored their food; They protected each other.
No: They should have been prepared/had more food and water with them; Adeline was frightened of the orcas; Adeline had to help her father)*

Score: ☐

Total Score: ☐

GOLD BAND Benchmark Assessment

Benchmark Assessment Summary

LOST AT SEA

NAME:

CLASS GROUP:

DATE:

Accuracy:

☐ **HARD**
Errors: more than 1:10

☐ **INSTRUCTIONAL**
Errors: between 1:10 and 1:25

☐ **EASY**
Errors; fewer than 1:25

Summary of Observations during the assessment

Reading Strategies:

Using Print:

Fluency:

Summary of Reading Comprehension Skills

Retelling the story:

Comprehension:

Recalling: ☐ / 2   Inferring: ☐ / 3   Responding: ☐ / 3   Total Score: ☐ / 8

Comments:

Recommendations:

Move to White Band? Y/N

112

Copyright © UCL Institute of Education and Cambridge University Press

WHITE BAND Benchmark Assessment

Error ratio:

Orientation for assessment:
'Cheng left his home and village behind and joined the merchants and travellers on the Silk Road. Will he find a new home?'

Accuracy rate:

Self correction ratio:

PAGE	TITLE: The Silk Road BAND: White	ERRORS	S/C	ERROR analysis			S/C analysis		
				M	S	V	M	S	V
8	Nobody on the road took much notice of Cheng, and he was happy with that. Some of the people were Chinese, but many weren't. They wore strange clothes and spoke strange languages, and a few rode strange animals.								
9	After a while, Cheng saw an inn at the side of the road. A rich man gave Cheng a silver coin to keep an eye on his horse while he went inside. Cheng spent it on a hot meal.								
10	That night, Cheng slept in the warm straw of the stables behind the inn. Over the next few days, he earned more silver coins. He kept an eye on the horses of rich men, he carried bags, he cleared tables for the innkeeper.								

Copyright © UCL Institute of Education and Cambridge University Press

		ERRORS	S/C	ERROR analysis			S/C analysis		
				M	S	V	M	S	V
11	Eventually, the innkeeper said he could sleep in a store room. 'Just watch out for the rats,' he said. Cheng made his corner as comfortable as he could. But it didn't feel like home.								
12	Time passed, and Cheng earned his silver coins, but he felt restless. One day, he got talking to an old man. 'There's more to life than this dirty little inn, you know,' said the old man. 'You can find anything on the Silk Road.'								
13	Perhaps the old man is right, Cheng thought. It was time to move on. So the very next morning, he packed a bag, said goodbye to the innkeeper and set off. He didn't look back.								

		ERRORS	S/C	ERROR analysis			S/C analysis		
				M	S	V	M	S	V
14	There were other inns, of course, and more silver coins to be earned. He looked after horses, guarded wagons, spent whole nights watching the goods for the merchants. But Cheng was also learning about trading. He saw how the best merchants haggled and made deals, so he did the same. 'You want me to keep an eye on your horse?' he said. 'Well, it's one silver coin for the first hour, then two for the next hour …' 'You strike a hard bargain, boy,' the rich merchants replied. But they always paid, because Cheng always did a good job.								
16	There were other things to be learned on the Silk Road. Cheng learned many new languages. Before long, he could talk to merchants in their own tongues and making deals became even easier.								
	Stop taking the running record at this point. Ask the child to read on quietly to themselves until the end of the story before beginning the comprehension assessment tasks.								
No of words **322**	**TOTALS** Total the sources of information used in self corrections and errors.								

Copyright © UCL Institute of Education and Cambridge University Press

WHITE BAND Benchmark Assessment
Comprehension assessment
The Silk Road

NAME:

CLASS GROUP:

DATE:

Retelling task: *(Tick and comment as appropriate)*

Retold independently. ☐

Retold using the pictures to support ☐

Retold with some adult support ☐

Sequencing Ideas: *(Tick and comment as appropriate)*

Followed the correct sequence of events ☐

Mentioned some of the events in sequence ☐

Events retold out of sequence ☐

Control of Vocabulary: *(Tick and comment as appropriate)*

Used vocabulary of the book and their own vocabulary appropriately and interchangeably ☐

Used the vocabulary of the book appropriately ☐

Unfocused or inaccurate use of vocabulary denoting lack of understanding ☐

Questioning to assess understanding *(Tick as appropriate)*

Recalling: 2

Tell me how Cheng earned his silver coins. ☐
(He looked after horses; He helped the innkeeper; He carried bags.)
What did Cheng do to help Haroun and Amina? ☐
(Watched out for the robbers; Woke them up when the robbers came; Joined in the fight to save their goods.)

Score: ☐

Inferring: 3

Why do you think nobody took any notice of Cheng when he joined the travellers (page 8)? ☐
(They were too busy to notice; There were so many people; Nobody knew who they could trust;
So new people joined all the time.)
The author tells us Cheng 'didn't look back' on page 13. What do you think the author means by this? ☐
(Cheng is not sorry to be leaving; He has made his mind up; He is ready to move on.)
What did Cheng do to make sure he wasn't robbed (page 18)? ☐
(Didn't trust anyone; Didn't make friends; Protected his money.)

Score: ☐

Responding: 2

What do you think Cheng means when he says 'You want me to keep an eye on your horse?' (page 14)? ☐
(He is offering to look after it while the owner is busy; He is asking if the owner wants him to mind the horse.)
Did you like this story? Can you tell me why/why not? (seek rationales for children's responses) ☐
(Yes: It was exciting; It had a happy ending; The illustrations matched the pictures well;
I liked the language the author used to make it exciting.)
(No: I found it a bit scary; I was sad when Cheng had to leave his home; I thought the author used some hard words/sentences.)

Score: ☐

Total Score: ☐

WHITE BAND Benchmark Assessment
Benchmark Assessment Summary
The Silk Road

NAME:

CLASS GROUP:

DATE:

Accuracy:

☐ **HARD**
Errors: more than 1:10

☐ **INSTRUCTIONAL**
Errors: between 1:10 and 1:25

☐ **EASY**
Errors; fewer than 1:25

Summary of Observations during the assessment

Reading Strategies:

Using Print:

Fluency:

Summary of Reading Comprehension Skills

Retelling the story:

Comprehension:

Recalling: ☐ / 2   Inferring: ☐ / 3   Responding: ☐ / 2   Total Score: ☐ / 7

Comments:

Recommendations:

Move to Conventional Stage? Y / N

Copyright © UCL Institute of Education and Cambridge University Press